教甄必考版

英語詞彙
語意邏輯
解題法

莫建清、楊智民、黃怡君
合著

線上影音精解：113年教師甄試詞彙題
https://video.morningstar.com.tw/0170047/0170047.html

晨星出版

作者簡介

莫建清　字彙修辭權威大師

美國羅徹斯特大學（University of Rochester）語言學博士。國立政治大學英文系專任教授職退休，專長「構詞學」、「英語字源學」、「構詞學與英語教學」等。主編《三民實用英漢辭典》、《三民精解英漢辭典》；著有《英語詞彙語意邏輯解題法》、《音義聯想單字記憶法》。

楊智民　格林法則研究專家

國立員林家商應用英語科教師。著有《格林法則單字記憶法》、《字首、字根、字尾記憶法》、《英語詞彙語意邏輯解題法》、《心智圖單字記憶法》等。曾任國家教育研究院教科書審查委員及國營事業英語考科審題教師，並參與三民版 108 課綱普通型高中、技術型高中教科書撰寫。設計 Word Up 線上動畫課程「字根字首魔法學院」，致力於推廣數位化教材。

黃怡君　美國英語教學碩士

美國私立賓州大學（University of Pennsylvania）英語教學碩士，國立員林農工英語教師。曾參與三民書局技術型高中英語自學手冊與題庫之撰寫。

目次

作者簡介 2
給讀者的話 6

Chapter 1 詞彙語意邏輯解題法

解題流程圖 12
找關鍵詞的祕訣 13
四種類型的題目 20

Chapter 2 認識對比、反義結構：BUT 型

題型解說：
But 型【對比、反義結構（contrast: pointing out differences）】 22
上下文中的線索
　「反義語」的線索（antonym clue） 42
　「經驗」的線索（experience clue） 43
考古題測驗與解析 44
實戰練習 63

Chapter 3 認識因果關係：BECAUSE 型

題型解說：
Because 型【因果關係（cause and effect）】 68

上下文中的線索
　「因果關係」的線索（cause and effect clue） 86
　「推斷」的線索（inference clue） 86
考古題測驗與解析 87
實戰練習 106

Chapter 4　認識並列結構：AND 型

題型解說：
And 型【並列結構（equality of ideas）】
　如何翻譯 And 110
　分析並列結構（equality of ideas） 112
　其他應注意之處 113
上下文中的線索
　「定義」的線索（definition clue） 115
　「補充說明」的線索（explanation clue） 116
　「實例解釋」的線索（example clue） 119
考古題測驗與解析 122
實戰練習 142

Chapter 5　認識修飾語結構：MODIFIER 型

題型解說：
Modifier 型【修飾語結構（句中帶有修飾語，如形容詞、副詞等）】 146

- Ⓐ 同位語 146
- Ⓑ 分詞片語 149
- Ⓒ 主詞補語 151
- Ⓓ 形容詞 152
- Ⓔ 形容詞子句 152
- Ⓕ 關係副詞 153
- Ⓖ 介＋名（形容詞片語）............................. 156
- Ⓗ 副詞／副詞片語／副詞子句 156
- Ⓘ 表「比較」的副詞子句：比較要同類 156
- Ⓙ 八大類副詞子句 157
- Ⓚ 表「目的」的副詞子句 159

上下文中的線索
　「同義字／近義字」的線索
　　（synonym or near-synonym clue）................. 159
　「同位語」的線索（appositive clue）................. 160
　「重述」的線索（restatement clue）................. 163

考古題測驗與解析 164

實戰練習 193

參考書目 196

給讀者的話

　　許多在臺灣所舉辦的英語測驗詞彙題，難度不亞於 GRE 測驗，如教師甄試、後醫考試、高普考、國營事業、研究所入學考試等，其目的是為了選拔各領域的優秀人才。考生通常依靠自己的努力來應對這些考試，如做考古題練習、背誦生字，以期能在考場上表現傑出。遺憾的是，這些考生往往缺乏有系統的語意邏輯解題訓練，因此準備過程中倍感吃力，難以在競爭激烈的考試中脫穎而出。

　　以高中英語教師甄試為例，許多學校的缺額一經公告，就有數百名考生蜂擁而至，爭取寥寥數個名額。考生面對巨大壓力，遠赴各地應考，只為了爭取一份穩定的工作。根據教育部統計，110 學年正式教師的錄取率僅 4.29%，由於競爭激烈，這些測驗刻意設計較高難度題目以甄選合適人選。扣除申論題、命題實作、教案設計、英中互譯等評分主觀性強的題目，考生應該在選擇題奪得高分，才能取得先機。

　　此外，根據歷年數據，後醫學士的錄取率也僅 2%～5%，其英語測驗同樣不容易。不僅如此，每年通過高普考競爭公職的考生也面臨高難度英語測驗題，許多考生費盡心力還是無法攻克，感到力有未逮。以 112 年高普考為例，高考錄取率 15.54%，普考 12.57%，反映公職競爭之激烈。

　　這些考生為了在激烈的競爭中脫穎而出，投入大量時間學習英語，但成效卻未必理想。他們誤以為大量刷題、勤背單字就能獲得高分，卻忘了這些英語測驗的本質是在考閱讀的能力。由於缺乏解題方法的系統訓練，考生耗費許多時間在低層次背誦和機械式練習上，考試時無從下手，更遑論快速精確解題。

唯有考生認清這些考試的本質是考閱讀，才能在考試的表現上有所突破。總的來說，閱讀能力是一種綜合的認知技能，涉及語言理解、邏輯思維和知識應用等方面。研究閱讀的知名學者 Goodman（1967）所提出的觀點是：「閱讀是一種心理語言的猜測遊戲。」（Reading: A Psycholinguistic Guessing Game）閱讀者在閱讀過程中會運用自身的背景知識去猜測、推理和詮釋閱讀的字句或篇章，人類大腦在閱讀時會根據眼前所見和已有的知識進行詮釋。

閱讀是一個極度複雜的心智過程，在解題時，考生需仔細觀察填空句，基於語意邏輯尋找適當線索，推論可能的正確解答，最後將解答融入上下文中以驗證所猜的是否正確。美國英語教學界流行這句話：「卓越的語言學習者也是卓越的猜測者。他們不斷尋找意義的線索，熟練地運用這些線索作出合理的推測。舉例來說，涉及猜測的成功閱讀理解策略，包括使用單詞周遭的語境和使用語法線索來確定生詞的含義。」

（Good language learners are good guessers. They constantly search for clues to meaning and skillfully use these clues to make reasonable guesses. For example, successful reading comprehension strategies that involve guessing include using the context around the word and using grammar clues to determine the meaning of unknown words.）

法國哲學家笛卡爾曾說：「許多問題，只需依據常識與邏輯，就能得到正確答案。」可惜，台灣的英語學習者不敢猜，也不擅長猜，過分仰賴翻譯，卻忽視語境的線索，並缺乏邏輯思考的訓練，導致學習成效不盡理想。若學習者僅仰賴英譯中的解題方式，則每千題需翻

譯一千次，每萬題需翻譯一萬次。相對而言，經過語意邏輯解題法訓練過的考生，不論題目如何變化，皆能自信地找出正確答案。因此，閱讀和解決英語詞彙題並非單純死記單字所能達成，對於有效率的學習者而言，閱讀既是視覺的（用眼睛看字），也是非視覺的（用頭腦運用常識與邏輯）。

　　我們所擬定的《英語詞彙語意邏輯解題法》能彌補學習者長期缺乏語意邏輯訓練的不足，並具備以下創新的特色：

　　一、為了讓學習者快速領悟出題的脈絡，掌握快、狠、準的詞彙解題攻略，本書獨創以圖示方式呈現解題流程圖，並列出找關鍵詞的訣竅（參見 Chapter1）。特別強調探究解題語意的邏輯，包括如何透過關鍵詞揣摩句意，準確尋覓線索，並通過上下文語境驗證答案之正確性。根據句子語意及句型結構，本書將詞彙題型歸納為四大類：「But 型」、「Because 型」、「And 型」以及「Modifier 型」。讀者一旦辨識出題目所屬類別，即可著手尋找關鍵詞。尋覓關鍵詞之際，首要任務是找實詞，依序由動詞、形容詞（以及帶有 -ly 之副詞）、名詞展開。在找到可能的正確解答後，將其融入句子，核對是否達意並能承接上下文意符合語境。

　　二、本書的考古題測驗涵蓋教師甄試、後醫考試、高普考、國營事業、研究所入學考試的英語測驗題目，透過這些精心設計的考題，培養考生的邏輯思維和語文能力，也啓發考生利用既有的資訊去推理猜測未知的訊息，因此，把解題的認知過程分為四個步驟：（1）取樣

（2）預測（3）檢驗（4）確認。考生在解題過程中，也同時在訓練自己的邏輯思維，增強閱讀能力，加倍提升英語能力，面對真實世界時能運用得體的英語適切表情達意，必然指日可待。

　　三、本書不僅涵蓋詞彙，還將常見的單字用法和文法修飾概念整合其中，學習者有了這樣的基礎，無形中提高學習閱讀、翻譯、寫作的興趣與成效。過去學習者所學的句型常呈零散狀態，而本書透過四大類型的章節，使學習者能輕鬆找到相關的表達方式。以表示「因果關係」的從屬連接詞為例，其中包括 because、since、as 等，其因果關聯程度由強至弱排列為：because ＞ since ＞ as。此外，在表達「因果」關係時，最常用的對等連接詞為 for（表示「因」）和 so（表示「果」）。學習者詳細閱讀本書中的這些解說，不僅能複習文法句型，還能透過解題實踐，深入理解其背後的道理，帶來極具價值的學習收益。

　　總括而言，本書不僅是一本關於語意邏輯解題的寶典，而且也提供了考生解題所需的文法句型知識。書中所傳授的知識不僅適用於考試，也會激發學習者運用靈活思維去注意語言與意義之間的關係。本書內容聚焦於教師甄試、後醫考試、高普考、國營事業、研究所入學考試的測驗題目，然其中所介紹的方法和策略，幾乎適用於各類詞彙測驗，包括學測、統測、教育會考、多益測驗，以及 GRE 的語文推理測驗等。讀者只需熟習英語詞彙語意邏輯解題法，即便面對最艱鉅的考題，也能信心十足。閱讀本書後，讀者將具備「有根據的猜測」（educated guess）的能力，遠離「瞎猜」（wild guess）的困境。

我們期望讀者在使用本書時，能體驗到我們不同的想法，至於所談的觀念和方法，在教與學上是否有啓示作用，便端賴學習者評定了。在編寫本書時，我們力求盡善盡美，歷經多次校對，但疏漏、失誤或偏頗之處在所難免，懇請同道先進以及讀者不吝賜教、給予指正，俾於再版時修正。此外，本書有些觀點與例句來自參考書目，附在書後，在此謹向諸作者深表敬意與謝意。

莫建清
楊智民
黃怡大
　　謹誌

Chapter 1

詞彙語意邏輯解題法

各級考試所測驗的詞彙題，題型千變萬化，不可言喻，但萬變不離其宗，那就是正確的用詞選項原來就在題目上。為讓讀者快速掌握快、狠、準的詞彙解題攻略，先列出解題流程，圖示如下：

解題流程圖（Flowchart of problem solving）

略讀測驗文句，揣摩句意與語意屬性
Skim the context

↓

注意屬於哪一類題型：But 型、Because 型、And 型、Modifier 型
Identify question types

↓

找出題目中的特殊關鍵詞、轉折詞、同義詞、標點符號等
Look for clues / transitional words / synonyms / punctuation

↓

直接答題，每題不必花太多時間
Go check answer choices

↓

若找不到適當答案，逐一消去不太可能的答案
Use the process of elimination to eliminate implausible answers

↓

猜測
Guess wisely

找關鍵詞的祕訣

祕訣 1

　　解題時務必要找出題目中的否定關鍵詞像是 not, never, seldom, barely, rarely, no, less, without, scarcely, hardly, otherwise, rather than, by no means, anything but, free of。

祕訣 2

　　解題時最重要的關鍵詞，就是先找題目中的動詞。若是聯繫動詞（linking verbs）用來連接形容詞、名詞、名詞片語、介系詞片語、名詞子句等，作為主詞補語（subjective complement）以補足主詞意義上不足之處，關鍵詞應落在主詞補語上。

　　常用的聯繫動詞如下：be, become, get, go, grow, come, turn, run, fall, remain, stay, keep, seem, appear, look, sound, feel, smell, taste 等。

例1

Lucy { is / seems / looks } kind. 露西（看起來）很親切。

▶ 焦點在 kind，形容詞用作主詞補語

例2

Lucy { is / becomes } a teacher. 露西是（成了）一名老師。

▶ 焦點在 a teacher，名詞用作主詞補語

例3

John remained <u>a bachelor</u> all his life. 約翰終身未婚。

▶ 焦點在a bachelor，名詞用作主詞補語

例4

Roses smell <u>sweet</u>. 玫瑰花聞起來很香。

▶ 焦點在sweet，形容詞用作主詞補語

例5

The leaves are beginning to turn <u>red</u>. 葉子開始變紅。

▶ 焦點在red，形容詞用作主詞補語

祕訣3

　　若「形容詞＋名詞」組合而成的名詞片語擔任主詞補語，則關鍵詞應落在「形容詞」上。

例

Tom is a <u>naughty</u> boy. 湯姆是個頑皮的男孩。

▶ 名詞片語a naughty boy擔任主詞補語，關鍵詞落在形容詞naughty上

祕訣4

　　動詞為句子核心，除主詞（施事者）外，若使用完全及物動詞，其後要接受詞（受事者）；若使用不完全及物動詞（如call、consider），除受詞以外，還需要受詞補語（objective complement）以補足意義上的不足，這就形成整句語意的焦點，也就成了該句的關鍵詞。

14　Chapter 1　詞彙語意邏輯解題法

句型如下：

S + Vt + O + OC-noun

例

They called the girl <u>Lucy</u>. 他們叫這個女孩露西。

▶ 受詞補語就是語意的焦點

They considered Lucy <u>a good student</u>. 他們認為露西是位好學生。

▶ 受詞補語就是語意的焦點

補語之前若要用介系詞 as，那只能與特定動詞搭配，像是 see, regard, recognize, rate, describe, take, portray, appoint, define, hail, characterize 等，其句型如下：

S + Vt + O + as + OC-noun

▶ 受詞補語就是語意的焦點

因與特定動詞搭配，這種題型，造型亮眼，超吸睛，英語學習者要特別留意。

祕訣5

若以句中動詞為中心的語意結構不可行時，應立即改成以形容詞為中心，其語境通常有下列二種，都以形容詞為解題的關鍵詞。

❶ be + adj.
❷ adj. + N

be 動詞雖然屬於高頻率的動詞，但語意模糊，隨文而變，不列入關鍵詞。

祕訣6

句中沒有形容詞為中心的語意結構,但有形容詞後面加 ly 組成的副詞,其後接形容詞、現在分詞或過去分詞,可列入解題的關鍵詞,其句型如下:

$$\text{adj.} + \text{ly} + \begin{Bmatrix} \text{adj.} \\ \text{participle} \end{Bmatrix}$$

祕訣7

only 與 even 都是解詞彙題的關鍵詞,要注意它們在句中的位置,因不同的位置會產生不同的句意。

例1

Adults　can swim　in the river　in the morning.
　S　　　V　　　adv. ph (place)　adv. ph (time)

大人早上可在河裡游泳。

說明

副詞 only 可插在上句中四個不同的位置,句義取決於組成成分之間的語意搭配。

❶ <u>Only</u> adults can swim in the river in the morning.
　▶ only修飾主詞adults,意指「只有大人可以游,小孩不行」

❷ Adults can <u>only</u> swim in the river in the morning.
　▶ only修飾動詞swim,意指「大人只可游泳,不可釣魚」

❸ Adults can swim <u>only</u> in the river in the morning.
　▶ only修飾表「地點」的副詞片語in the river,意指「大人只可在河裡游泳,不可在湖裡游泳」

❹ Adults can swim in the river <u>only</u> in the morning.
▶ only修飾表「時間」的副詞片語in the morning，意指「大人只可在早上游泳，其他時間都不行」

注意 中文說「只有」，同學常譯成「only have」，如下列：
✗ I <u>only</u> have one son. 【only修飾have】
○ I have <u>only</u> one son. 【only修飾one】
我只有一個兒子。

例2

Robert　was hurt.
　S　　　 V
羅伯特受傷了。

說明

副詞 even 意思是「連……，甚至……」，用於強調「沒想到、出乎意外」，可插在上句兩個不同的位置，句義取決於組成成分之間的語意搭配，詞彙學習者有時要融入情境裡，才能領會作者的弦外之音。

❶ Robert was <u>not even</u> hurt. (He was quite all right.)
▶ not even修飾動詞was hurt。語境是：羅伯特騎機車上台北市南京西路，途中不慎跌入天坑，被人救起後，出乎意外<u>羅伯特甚至連受傷都沒有</u>，也就是毫髮無傷

❷ <u>Not even</u> Robert was hurt. (All were safe.)
▶ not even修飾主詞Robert。語境是：羅伯特因小腿關係不良於行，某天在路上突遇地震，不慎跌倒，出乎意外，<u>甚至連羅伯特都沒有受傷</u>，言外之意，其餘的人都安全了

以上❶❷兩例出自金陵（2008:227）。

祕訣8

　　副詞、副詞片語、副詞子句，如同一般的修飾語，要找出關鍵詞——誰是被修飾者？是動詞，是形容詞或是副詞呢？

祕訣9

　　分詞片語放在句首的位置，修飾句中的關鍵詞：主要句子的主詞（如例 1 的主詞 Ancient Athens），而副詞子句放在句首的位置，則修飾句中的關鍵詞：主要句子的動詞（如例 2 的動詞 is said）。

例1

(Being) known for its early development of the democratic system, Ancient Athens is often said to be the cradle of democracy.
因民主制度早期的發展而聞名，古雅典常常被譽為民主的搖籃。

例2

Because Ancient Athens is known for its early development of the democratic system, it is often said to be the cradle of democracy.
因民主制度早期的發展而聞名，古雅典常常被譽為民主的搖籃。

注意

❶ 在統測、學測、指考、教甄、研究所的考題裡，句首的分詞片語的句意幾乎都是表「原因」。

❷ 出現在句首的分詞片語是由副詞子句簡化而成。（詳情請參見 149 頁 ❸ 分詞片語）

❸ 有時分詞片語中沒出現分詞,只見形容詞(如例 1 的 known for),那是因句子簡潔緣故,being 被省略了。
❹ 出現在句中其他位置的分詞片語,大多是由形容詞子句簡化而成,修飾該子句前面的名詞先行詞。

祕訣10

若有不同認知概念的單詞或片語,隱含負面概念,或隱含「貶」的意味,常加單引號(' ')或雙引號(" "),照字面意義翻譯成中文需加「」。比如你與對方對 art 有不同認知概念,譯成中文「藝術」,隱含對藝術有貶的意味,如「什麼藝術、爛藝術、藝術個鬼」。

祕訣11

另外,「distinguished / known / reputation for」皆意指「因某事而知名」。這些片語中的介系詞 for 用於表示「原因」,其後通常接與「原因」相關的解題關鍵字。

祕訣12

這是最後但並非最不重要的一點 (last but not least),每個應試者牢記所選的詞彙正確答案,一定要以句子語意的相關性為前提,符合題目所設的語境,並非先在四個選項裡挑來挑去,只看表層意思未能探究其深層意義,而挑出「自我感覺良好」的錯誤答案。總之,解詞彙題務必斟酌上下文語境並尋找語境的線索,因而最重要的關鍵詞是線索和語境,掌握這些關鍵詞,考生才能玩弄考題於股掌之間,才能躲開「請君入甕」或「誘人入罪」的困擾答案。

四種類型的題目（four types of questions）

❶ But 型【對比、反義結構（contrast: pointing out differences）】
　▶ 詳情請參閱 Chapter 2
❷ Because 型【因果關係（cause and effect）】
　▶ 詳情請參閱 Chapter 3
❸ And 型【並列結構（equality of ideas）】
　▶ 詳情請參閱 Chapter 4
❹ Modifier 型【修飾語結構（句中帶有修飾語，如形容詞、副詞等）】▶ 詳情請參閱 Chapter 5

Chapter 2

認識對比、反義結構：

BUT 型

題型解說

But 型【對比、反義結構（contrast: pointing out differences）】

　　本章節要介紹的是 But 型，對等連接詞 but 不一定要譯成中文「但是」，連接兩個對等子句時，除了特別短的句子外，通常在第一個句子末尾，也就是 but 前面會加一個逗號（,）表示稍停。

$$\text{正}\oplus \qquad\qquad \text{負}\ominus$$
$$(,)\left\{\mathbf{but}\right\}$$
$$\text{負}\ominus \qquad\qquad \text{正}\oplus$$

說明

　　表「對比、反義」的 But 型，句子含義會顯示出「正、負」相對的語意屬性，通常有對比關係指的是反義關係。譬如，句中用反義連接詞（adversative conjunction）but，表示連接前後兩個部分的語意是表「對比」或「相反」。換言之，一個是正向意義，另一個必須是負向意義，反之亦然。

例1

John is very <u>poor</u> (負) but (he is) very <u>honest</u> (正).
約翰雖窮，但很老實。

例2

The spirit is <u>willing</u> (正), but the flesh is <u>weak</u> (負).
心有餘而力不足；力不從心。
▶ spirit與flesh：名詞對比。willing與weak：形容詞對比

例3

Speech is <u>silver</u> (負), but silence is <u>golden</u> (正).
說話是銀，沉默是金。
▶ speech與silence：名詞對比。silver（銀，價低）與golden（金，價高）：形容詞對比

例4

He <u>likes</u> (正) classical music, but I <u>don't</u> (負).
他喜歡古典音樂，（但）我可不喜歡。 ▶「但」可省略不譯

例5

This old hotel is <u>commodious</u> (正) but <u>not</u> particularly <u>attractive</u> (負)；its big lobby is filled with artwork and old furniture.
這家老旅館雖寬敞但並不特別吸引人；其大廳擺滿了藝術品和老家具。

現再列舉其他這類型的標示詞如下：

· but	· given (prep.)	· A be in contrast to B
· although	· only to	· initially A...eventually B
· albeit (=although)	· except	· formerly A now B
▶古語	· whereas	· compare A with B
· in spite of	· while (=although)	= A be compared with B
· despite	· in fact (=actually)	· once...now...
· for all	· in reality (=actually)	· from A to B

· even though	· in truth	· nonetheless
· even if	（=truly, in fact)	▶多用於書面語體
· on the other hand	· in practice	· nevertheless
· on the contrary	（=in reality)	▶多用於書面語體
· yet	· unlike (prep.)	· notwithstanding
▶多用於口頭語體	· turn (=transform)	(prep., adv.)
· instead of	A into B	▶多用於書面語體
· instead (adv.)	▶A、B不同類	· however
· no surprise	· not A but rather B	· normally (now)
· surprising	· A rather than B	· differ from
· unexpected	· by contrast /	(=be different from)
· ironically	in contrast	· as opposed to
· unfortunately	· far from	(=in contrast to)
· not necessarily	· apart from	· the other way around
（=not always）	· alternate between	(= the opposite of what is
· the more...the	A and B	expected)
less...	· whether A or B	

例1

$\begin{Bmatrix} \text{Although} \\ \text{Whereas} \\ \text{While} \end{Bmatrix}$ Mary loses her temper **quickly** (負),
Peter **seldom** does (正).

瑪莉常勃然大怒，彼得卻很少勃然大怒。

> **說明**
>
> 從屬連接詞 although 或 though（雖然）引導一個表「讓步」的副詞子句，用於修飾主要子句的動詞（does），讓這兩個子句的語境形成「對比或對照」。

例 2

Stone (2007) coined the term "continuous partial attention" and distinguished it from multitasking. She wrote that multitasking is driven by a desire to be more productive whereas "continuous partial attention" means, literally, to pay partial attention–continuously.

史東（2007）創造了「持續性局部注意力」這個術語，並將其與多重任務處理區分開來。她寫道，多重任務處理的驅力是來自想要更有成效的渴望，而「持續性局部注意力」字面上意味著付出部分的注意力──持續地。

例 3

Although he won the lottery, (正) Peter soon _____ away millions he won within a year (負).

Ⓐ fabricated　　**Ⓑ** frittered　　**Ⓒ** emulated　　**Ⓓ** incapacitated

雖然彼得中了樂透，但他在一年內很快就揮霍掉了他贏得的數百萬元。

　　fritter 是個語意表義的生詞，fr- 表「摩擦」、「磨損」，金錢越磨越少。（欲知更多 fr- 語音表義的例子，請參考《音義聯想單字記憶法》p. 176。）

答案：B

例 4

But even if many single pieces of knowledge are still missing, the main structure of the relationship can be discerned without too much difficulty.

但即使許多單一知識片段仍然缺失，主要的關係結構仍然可以毫不困難地辨識出來。

例5

$$\begin{Bmatrix} \text{Despite} \\ \text{For all} \\ \text{In spite of} \end{Bmatrix} \text{his wealth (正), he is not happy (負).}$$

=Although he is wealthy (正), he is not happy (負).
他雖富有，但並不快樂。

說明

可用對比式的轉折介系詞 despite（雖然、儘管）或介系詞片語 for all 或 in spite of，後面接上受詞來代替連接詞 though 或 although 所引導的副詞子句。

例6

❶ 對等連接詞 but
　👎 John was very tired, but he kept on working.
　👍 Although John was very tired, he kept on working.
　　約翰很疲倦，但仍繼續工作。

說明

用對等連接詞 but 連接兩個獨立子句，表示兩個子句不分輕重，表達的意思一視同仁。事實上，兩句話的重點在第二句「他仍繼續工作」，因此英譯應以此句為主要子句。

❷ 連繫副詞 however

    a) John was very tired; however, he kept on working.

    b) John was very tired; he, however, kept on working.

    c) John was very tired; he kept on working, however.

    d) John was very tired. However, he kept on working.

    約翰非常疲倦，然而他仍然繼續工作。

說明

純連接詞（pure conjunction），如 but, and, so 等只能出現在第二句的句首，而連繫副詞（conjunctive adverb）可以移位，可以出現在第二個句子的句首、句中或句尾。兩個句子之間，常用分號（semicolon）或句號（period）隔開，連繫副詞後也常用逗號（comma）。試比較上例 but 與 however。另兩個連繫副詞 nevertheless, nonetheless 的用法與 however 的用法相類似。

例7

Life seems exciting, novel, fascinating, and stimulating. However, after a while, the newness and strangeness of being in another country can influence emotions in an exotic way.

生活似乎令人興奮、新奇、迷人且刺激。然而，過了一段時間，身處異國的新奇和陌生感可能會以一種奇特的方式影響情緒。

例8

   ✗ Although John was not much interested in music, but he attended the concert.

   ○ ❶ Although John was not much interested in music, he attended the concert.

   ○ ❷ John was not much interested in music, but he attended the concert.

      雖然約翰對音樂沒太多興趣，但還是出席了音樂會。

> **說明**
>
> 英文只能有一個主要子句（S+V），所以要遵守「主從分明」的原則。如果從屬連接詞 although 與對等連接詞 but 同時出現，就分不清楚誰主、誰從，所以英文裡不能同時把 although、but 用在同一個句子裡。同理類推，英文裡也不能有 because..., so... 這樣的句子。

例9

John loves crowds; Mary { , however, / , on the other hand, / , in contrast, } is fond of solitude.

約翰喜歡合群，而瑪莉卻喜歡孤獨。

例10

English speakers are sanguine about homophony, making little attempt to clarify meanings, <u>while</u> Chinese speakers, <u>on the other hand</u>, seem to have a more sensitive radar for ambiguity.

英文使用者對同音異形異義詞持正向態度，很少努力澄清含義，而相反地，中文使用者則似乎對歧義有更敏銳的感知。

例11

Fleeing the family nest is a rite of passage many teenagers dream of, <u>yet</u> it's a luxury millennials and Generation Z across much of the Western world are having to wait much longer for.

離開家庭是許多青少年夢寐以求的成年禮，但對於西方世界許多地區的千禧世代和Z世代來說，現在卻是必須花更長時間等待的奢望。

註 Generation Z也被成為Net Generaion（網路世代）。

例12

His mood <u>alternates between</u> joy (正) and despair (負).
他悲喜交加。

例13

John's marks, <u>by contrast with</u> Peter's, were excellent.
與彼得的分數相比較，約翰的分數太好了。

例14

An all-electric Chevrolet Bolt, for instance, can be expected to produce 189 grams of carbon dioxide for every mile driven over its lifetime. <u>By contrast,</u> a new gasoline-fueled Toyota Camry is estimated to produce 385 grams of carbon dioxide per mile.
例如，一輛全電動的雪佛蘭Bolt，在其使用壽命內，每行駛一英里可預期產生189克二氧化碳。相比之下，一輛新的汽油動力的豐田凱美瑞估計每英里產生385克二氧化碳。

例15

In rich countries, there was a vast surplus of food. More often than not their people threw away food at will. <u>In contrast,</u> some impoverished countries seemed unable to benefit from the green revolution. 富裕國家有大量的過剩食物。他們的人民往往隨意丟棄食物。對比之下，一些貧困的國家似乎無法從綠色革命中受益。

例16

John seems to consider the matter trivial; it is, <u>on the contrary</u>, very serious. 約翰似乎認為那事件微不足道，恰恰相反，它是很嚴重的。

注意 切勿混淆on the contrary（恰恰相反）和on the other hand（在另一方面）。

例17

$$\left\{\begin{array}{l}\text{Unlike}\\ \text{Contrary to}\\ \text{As opposed to}\end{array}\right\} \text{Los Angeles, New York doesn't have earthquakes.}$$

不像洛杉磯，紐約沒有地震。

例18

A habit is not easily shaken off, whether it is **good** or **bad**.
習慣不易改掉，不管是好習慣或是壞習慣。

> **說明**
>
> whether...or... 所引導表示讓步的副詞子句，其意為「不論是否……；不管是……或是……」。

例19

Philosophical debates have arisen over the use of technology, with disagreements over <u>whether</u> technology improves the human condition <u>or</u> worsens it.
科技的使用引發了哲學上的爭論，人們對技術是否改善了人類狀況，還是使其惡化，存在分歧。

例20

<u>Given</u> their inexperience, they have done a good job.
若考慮到他們缺乏經驗，他們已把工作做得很好了。

> **說明**
>
> 　　Given 作介系詞用，意思是「如果把……考慮在內（if we take into account）」。

例21

Given that many students struggle with maintaining focused attention, particularly when reading textbooks, it can be anticipated that they will look for stimulation, whether or not it is relevant to their learning.
如果考慮到許多學生難以保持專注，特別是在閱讀教科書時，可以預期他們會找尋刺激，無論這些刺激是否與他們的學習有關。

> **說明**
>
> 　　given that S + V 中的 given 做連接詞用。given 本是過去分詞，但也可以當作介系詞和連接詞用，意思是「（如果）考慮到（considering a particular thing, or considering that）」，Randolph Quirk、Sidney Greenbaum、Geoffrey Leech 和 Jan Svartvik 所著的《英語綜合語法》（*A Comprehensive Grammar of the English Language*）舉了幾個例子說明，摘錄如下：
>
> ❶ Given the present conditions, I think she's done really well.
> 　如果考慮到目前的情況，我認為她做得非常出色。
>
> 　　此處的 given 雖是以過去分詞的型態呈現，但用法上卻是介系詞，和一般介系詞用法相同。像 including, excluding, concerning, regarding, considering, given 這種看似分詞的介系詞，具有和一般介系詞相同的語法功能，後面加受詞。這種型態和一般介系詞不同的介系詞叫做「邊緣介系詞」（marginal prepositions）。

> ❷ <u>Given that</u> this work was produced under particularly difficult circumstances, the reuslt is better than could be expected.
> 如果考慮到這份工作是在特別困難的環境下完成的，結果比預期的要好。
>
> 此處的 given 當從屬連接詞用，引導副詞子句 <u>Given that</u> this work was produced under particularly difficult circumstances 修飾主要子句的形容詞 better than could be expected。

例22

If the Taiwan of today <u>is compared with</u> the Taiwan of yesterday, we see what a change we have effected!
今日的台灣和過去的台灣比一比，就可以看出我們已經產生多大的改變！

> **說明**
>
> 根據 Strunk & White 編撰的英語寫作教材 *The Elements of Style* 對 compare A with B 所下的定義：
>
> To compare with is mainly to point out differences between objects regarded as essentially of the same order.
> 也就是「比較」或「相較」A、B 間的差異，點出兩者間不同之處。

例23

<u>Compared with</u> misery, happiness is relatively unexplored terrain for social scientists. Between 1967 and 1994, 46380 articles indexed in *Psychological Abstracts* mentioned depression, 36851 anxiety, and

5099 anger. Only 2389 spoke of happiness, 2340 life satisfaction, and 405 joy.

相較於痛苦，快樂對社會科學家而言是個相對未探索的領域。在1967年至1994年之間，編入《心理學摘要》索引的 46380 篇文章提到了憂鬱，36851 篇文章提到了焦慮，5099 篇文章提到了憤怒。只有 2389 篇文章提到了幸福，2340 篇文章提到了生活滿意度，405 篇文章提到了喜悅。

例24

Perry enjoyed the actor's nuanced performance, especially compared to the previous actor who was loud and too dramatic.
佩瑞喜歡這位演員細緻入微的表演，特別是與之前那位吵鬧且過度戲劇化的演員相比。

說明

　　compare A to B 是找出 A 和 B 之間的相似性，進而將 A 比喻為 B，例如莎士比亞《十四行詩・18》的名句：Shall I compare thee to a summer's day?（我是否可以把你比喻為夏日呢？），莎士比亞透過修辭性的問句說他是否可以把一位年輕的少年比喻為夏日。至於 compare A with B 是用以尋找 A 和 B 的差異性，例如：When you compare the efficiency of the old system with that of the new one, the difference is quite remarkable.（拿舊系統的效率和新系統比較，差異相當顯著。）

　　不過，在美式英語裡，compare A to B 有時可以用以比較兩者之間的差異，用法和 compare A with B 沒有差異，《遠東新世紀英漢辭典》舉了一個例子說明兩者用法沒有差異：The earth is only a baby (when it is) compared with [to] many other celestial bodies.（和許多其他天體比較起來，地球只不過是個嬰兒〔只是小巫見大巫〕。）因此，例 24 的 compared to 意同於 compared with。

例25

New York, which was <u>once</u> a small town, <u>now</u> has eight million people.
紐約過去是個小鎮，如今已有八百萬人口。

例26

While her sister <u>went</u> to Oxford, she now <u>goes</u> to Cambridge.
她姐姐從前到牛津念書，她現在卻到劍橋求學。

> **說明**
>
> while 有對比的意味，可從所使用的時態不同看出（went, goes）。

例27

While not completely nonplussed by the unusually caustic responses from members of the audience, the speaker was nonetheless visibly _____ by their lively criticism.

Ⓐ humiliated　　**Ⓑ** tantalized　　**Ⓒ** deluded　　**Ⓓ** discomfited

儘管演講者對聽眾異常刻薄的反應沒有完全感到不知所措，但仍然對他們激烈批評感到明顯的不安。

答案：D

例28

Upon the super typhoon warning, Nancy rushed to the supermarket—<u>only to</u> find the shelves almost bare and the stock nearly gone.
超級颱風警報一發佈，南西就趕往超市，卻發現貨架上幾乎空無一物（bare），幾乎沒東西可買了。

> 說明

❶ Only to + verb 意思是「結果出乎意料；反而；結果卻」。可表結果，修飾其前的動詞。

> 例

John studied hard <u>only to</u> fail.
= John studied hard but he failed.
約翰很用功，結果卻失敗了。

▶ only to fail修飾其前的動詞studied的結果

❷ 介系詞upon意思是「（在某事發生時）一……就」
▶ 相當於連接詞片語as soon as

> 例

<u>Upon</u> his arrival home, he switched on the TV.
= <u>As soon as</u> he arrived home, he switched on the TV.
他一到家就打開電視。

例29

Living with alopecia from the age of 10, Rowlands has found herself a target of bullying. As a child she wore wigs and hats, <u>only to</u> have other children steal them and throw them into gardens.

羅蘭斯自10歲起就與脫髮症共存，發現自己成為欺凌的目標。在童年時期，她戴著假髮和帽子，卻經常被其他孩子偷走，扔進花園。

例30

<u>Notwithstanding</u> some financial problems (=<u>In spite of</u> some financial problems), he still bought a car of his own.

儘管有些財務問題，他還是買了屬於自己的車。

> **說明**
>
> notwithstanding 多用於書面語體，可以做介系詞，其意為「雖然、儘管」（in spite of）。

例31

Also, during autumn, deciduous trees drop their leaves and grow them again in spring. <u>Nonetheless</u>, the most common biological rhythm is the circadian one, which happens once a day.

此外，在秋天落葉樹會落葉，在春天再次長出新葉。然而，最常見的生物節奏是晝夜節律，每 24 小時發生一次。

例32

With multinational attacks, terrorism today has truly reached a global scale. It now aims for targets on a transnational scale <u>instead of</u> local.

隨著跨國攻擊事件的發生，今日恐怖主義已真正達到全球規模。現在鎖定的是跨國的目標，而不限於本地。

例33

Their first suggestion is for educators to approach the Ukraine war as learners. Teachers do <u>not necessarily</u> have to be scholars or researchers of Russia's invasion of Ukraine to effectively teach it. <u>Instead</u>, they should frame themselves as learners who utilize their experiences of being learners transparently and as a form of modeling.

他們的第一個建議是讓教育者以學習者的身份探討烏克蘭戰爭。教師不一定要是研究俄羅斯入侵烏克蘭的學者或研究者，才能有效地教授這個主題。相反地，他們應該直接利用自己作為學習者的經歷，將自己定位為學習者，並以自己作為一種模範。

> 說明

　　instead 的詞性是副詞，意思是「代替、頂替、反而、卻」，通常置於句首或句末。

❶ John never watches TV. <u>Instead</u>, he watches his bird all day long.
約翰從不看電視，而是整天看他的鳥。

❷ Sarah couldn't attend the meeting, so I went <u>instead</u>.
莎拉不能參加會議，所以我代她去了。

　　instead of 的詞性是介系詞，後加名詞或動名詞，意思是「代替；作為……的替換；而不是」，可置於句首或句中。

❶ <u>Instead of</u> taking the elevator, they decided to climb the stairs for some exercise.
他們不搭電梯，決定爬樓梯當運動。

❷ He opted for a healthy salad <u>instead of</u> a greasy burger for lunch.
他選擇了健康的沙拉，而不是油膩的漢堡作為午餐。

例 34

Companies tend to favor national rules, <u>rather than</u> be forced to deal with a patchwork of local laws.
公司往往偏好國家層面的法規，而不是被迫應對零碎的地方法律。

例35

The authors are <u>not</u> suggesting that Shakespeare plagiarized <u>but rather</u> that he read and was inspired by a manuscript titled "A Brief Discourse of Rebellion and Rebels," written in the late 1500s by George North, a minor figure in the court of Queen Elizabeth.

作者不是在暗示莎士比亞抄襲，而是認為他讀過一份名為《叛亂與叛亂者的簡要論述》的手稿而得到啟發，該手稿為16世紀晚期的伊莉莎白女王宮廷中的小角色喬治・諾斯所著。

例36

<u>Unlike</u> traditional psychology that focuses more on the negative aspects of life such as healing traumas, Positive Psychology emphasizes the importance of building positive emotions and experiences to boost human strengths and lead human beings to thrive.

不同於傳統心理學更聚焦於生活的負面方面，如療癒創傷，正向心理學強調建立正向情緒和經驗的重要性，以提升人類的優勢，引領人類茁壯成長。

例37

Australia closed its borders to almost everyone <u>except</u> citizens and residents in March 2020 in an attempt to slow surging COVID-19 case numbers.

澳大利亞於2020年3月關閉邊境，僅允許公民和居民入境，以減緩激增的COVID-19病例數。

例38

The paradox of meritocracy builds on other research showing that those who think they are the most objective can <u>actually</u> exhibit the most bias in their evaluations.

精英主義的悖論建立在其他研究之上，這些研究表明，那些認為自己最客觀的人，其評價實際上可能會表現出最大的偏見。

例39

These key areas include many major cities where baboons are seemingly abundant. In reality, baboon numbers are dropping.

這些最主要地區包括許多看起來有大量狒狒的大城市。但事實上，狒狒的數量正在下降。

例40

Some zoo supporters say that captive animals serve as conservation 'ambassadors' for their wild counterparts, and that zoos are a 'Noah's Ark' that provides a buffer against the decline of endangered species. In truth, however, this is a script that even the zoo industry has quietly abandoned.

一些動物園的支持者表示，圈養的動物可以充當其野生同類的保育「大使」，而動物園則是「諾亞方舟」，為瀕危物種的減少提供緩衝。然而，實際上，這是一個連動物園業界都悄悄放棄的一個腳本。

例41

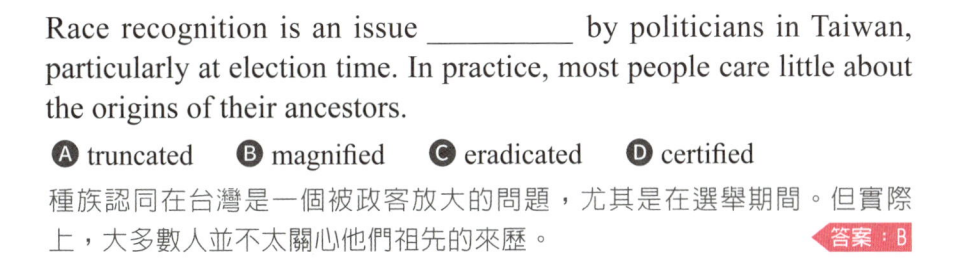

Race recognition is an issue _____ by politicians in Taiwan, particularly at election time. In practice, most people care little about the origins of their ancestors.

Ⓐ truncated　Ⓑ magnified　Ⓒ eradicated　Ⓓ certified

種族認同在台灣是一個被政客放大的問題，尤其是在選舉期間。但實際上，大多數人並不太關心他們祖先的來歷。

答案：B

例42

According to legend, the philosopher's stone was a substance that could <u>turn</u> ordinary metals like iron, tin, lead, zinc, nickel or copper <u>into</u> precious metals like gold and silver.

根據傳說，賢者之石是一種能夠將普通金屬（如鐵、錫、鉛、鋅、鎳或銅）轉化為貴金屬（如金和銀）的物質。

例43

They tried every effort to transform adversity into _____ and to turn something of less value into something of high value.

Ⓐ credibility　　**Ⓑ** opportunity　　**Ⓒ** meditation　　**Ⓓ** promotion

他們盡一切努力將逆境轉化為機遇，將價值較低的東西轉化為價值較高的東西。

答案：B

例44

<u>Far from</u> being a bug, ambiguity is a useful feature for languages. It allows us to create ample vocabularies by recycling some of the most common and easy-to-pronounce clumps of sound.

歧義絕非語言的缺陷，而是一個有用的特徵。這讓我們能夠透過重新利用一些最常見且容易發音的音叢，創造豐富的詞彙。

例45

AD / HD is a neurological disorder which stems <u>not</u> from the <u>home</u> environment, but from biological and genetic causes.

「注意力不足或過動症」是一種神經性疾病，其根源不是來自家庭環境，而是源自生物和遺傳性因素。

例46

"Deep reading"—as opposed to the often superficial reading we do on the Web—is an endangered practice, one we ought to take steps to preserve as we would a significant work of art.

「深度閱讀」——不同於我們在網上經常進行的膚淺閱讀——是一種瀕臨絕跡的做法，我們應該像保護重要的藝術品一樣，採取措施來保存它。

例47

In some Asian countries, the meaning of "self-learning" for high school students may differ from what we might expect.

在某些亞洲國家，高中生對於「自學」的含義，可能與我們的預期有所不同。

例48

Since men and women are segregated in the workplace, men tend not to value the work carried out by women, but not the other way around.

由於職場上存在性別隔離，男性往往不重視女性所做的工作，但反之則不然。

上下文中的線索

　　英語學習者是否能依據上下文推測出生詞的含義，取決於是否能找出文章中的詞彙或句構所提供常見的線索來幫助理解，而非單靠生詞或單字本身的意思，應以整句或整段的理解為主。這也是英美語言教學專家常說的話：A good reader can often figure out what new words mean by using context.（好的讀者通常可以通過上下文猜測出新的單詞的意思）。

「反義語」的線索（antonym clue）

　　在 But 類型的題目中，句中有些詞義與生詞的詞義相反，常常出現在表對比的連接詞、副詞或介系詞片語之後，提示對比關係，像是 although, but, however, while, by contrast, on the other hand, in contrast，或者在否定詞之後，像是 not, rarely, never, seldom, less, rather than, without, unlike，例如：

❶ Knowledge advances by steps, not by leaps.
　知識要循序漸進。

❷ The more haste, the less speed.
　欲速則不達。

❸ The less porridge, the more spoons.
　粥少僧多。

❹ Deeds, not words.
　重行動，不重空言。

❺ Fire and water are good servants, but (they are) bad masters.
　水能載舟，亦能覆舟。

❻ His dark brown jacket had holes in the elbows and had faded to light brown, <u>but</u> he continued to wear it.
他的深咖啡色夾克在手肘處有破洞,已經褪色成淺咖啡色,但他還是繼續穿。

▶ 此處it指誰?it指的是已褪成淺咖啡色的夾克

❼ What he lacks is <u>not</u> intelligence <u>but rather</u> perseverance.
他所缺的不是聰明才智而是毅力。

「經驗」的線索 (experience clue)

有時詞彙的搭配(lexical collocation)可以靠英語使用者的生活經驗去推測。例如:

❶ John and Peter went into the Chinese restaurant and a waitress brought them the <u>menu</u>.
約翰和彼得走進中餐廳,有一位女服務生給他們遞上了菜單。

❷ Generally speaking, the weather in Taiwan is hot and <u>humid</u> in summer.
一般而言,夏天台灣的天氣炎熱潮濕。

❸ After checking my throat, Dr. Young <u>prescribed</u> some medicine to me.
檢查完我的喉嚨後,楊醫師開了一些藥物給我。

考古題測驗與解析

Choose the answer that best completes each sentence below.

1. It comes as no surprise that societies have codes of behavior; the character of the codes, **on the other hand**, can often be _____.

Ⓐ predicable　Ⓑ unexpected　Ⓒ admirable　Ⓓ explicit
Ⓔ confusing

中譯	社會有行為規範並不令人意外，但規範的性質可能常出乎意料。 Ⓐ 可斷定的　Ⓑ 出乎意料的；想不到的 Ⓒ 可欽佩的；值得讚賞的　Ⓓ 清楚明白的；易於理解的 Ⓔ 難以理解的；不清楚的
取樣	瀏覽全文，藉標示詞on the other hand（在另一方面、反過來說）猜測前後句應呈現對比的意義，若有對比關係通常指的是反義關係。取樣前句含有否定詞no（不）的動詞片語comes as no surprise（並不令人意外）。
預測	後句的空格內應填入表示對比comes as no surprise（其意等同於is expected）的相反詞語，預測選項 Ⓑ unexpected（出乎意料的；想不到的）為可能答案。
檢驗	將 Ⓑ 選項填入空格中檢驗句意。
確認	瀏覽上下句，整體句意連貫，確認答案為 Ⓑ，正確答案就在題目上。

2. Steven was not able to finish his assignment on time, and, **instead of** being honest about it, he _____ an excuse in order to gain more time to complete it.

Ⓐ contemplated　Ⓑ dedicated　Ⓒ fabricated　Ⓓ stipulated

中譯	史蒂芬未能按時完成作業，他並沒有坦誠面對，反而編造藉口，以便獲得更多時間來完成作業。 Ⓐ 仔細考慮、熟慮（問題等）；沉思　Ⓑ 把……奉獻給 Ⓒ 編造；捏造　Ⓓ （條約或契約上）規定；明確要求
取樣	瀏覽全文，藉標示詞instead of（而非、而不是）猜測前後應呈現對比的意義，取樣動名詞片語being honest about it（坦誠面對）。
預測	空格內應填入表示對比具有「正面」含義的being honest about it的字詞，預測選項 Ⓒ fabricated（編造）為可能答案。學生未能完成作業，卻編造了一個藉口（fabricated an excuse），其目的是為了避免遭受老師懲罰或責罵，具有「負面」含義。
檢驗	將 Ⓒ 選項填入空格中檢驗句意。
確認	瀏覽上下句，整體句意連貫，確認答案為 Ⓒ，正確答案就在題目上。

3. Toward the end of the story "Beauty and the Beast" the fairy **turns** Beast **into** an <u>alluring</u>, handsome young man as promised.

　Ⓐ cholera　Ⓑ enduring　Ⓒ loathing　Ⓓ charismatic

中譯	在《美女與野獸》故事接近尾聲時，仙女履行諾言，將野獸變成了迷人英俊的年輕男子。 Ⓐ 霍亂　　　　　Ⓑ 持久的；耐久的 Ⓒ 憎恨；憎惡　Ⓓ 有超凡魅力的
取樣	瀏覽全文，藉標示詞turn A into B（使變成）猜測into前後A、B兩個對象應呈現對比或反義的意義，取樣擬人化的專有名詞Beast（野獸）。
預測	畫線處應該是和有「負面」含義的Beast表示對比的字詞，根據《美女與野獸》故事，野獸長得醜陋，缺乏魅力，因此答案需要和醜陋、缺乏魅力相反。此外，這個字要和alluring（迷人的；有吸引力的）意思接近（考同義字），預測選項 Ⓓ charismatic（有超凡魅力的）為可能答案。

檢驗	將 ❻ 選項代入畫線處檢驗句意。
確認	瀏覽上下句，整體句意連貫，確認答案為 ❻，正確答案就在題目上。

4. **Although** the period in which he lived represents the sunset of the Renaissance, Bernini possessed a _____ comparable to that of Leonardo or Michelangelo.

   Ⓐ chagrin　　Ⓑ virtuosity　　Ⓒ penchant　　Ⓓ gusto

中譯	雖然貝尼尼生活的時代，代表文藝復興時期的衰落，但他卻擁有與李奧納多或米開朗基羅相媲美的精湛技藝。 Ⓐ（因失敗犯錯等所產生之）失望；惱怒 Ⓑ 精湛技藝　Ⓒ 愛好；嗜愛 Ⓓ（做某事的）熱情；（個人的）喜好；藝術的風格
取樣	瀏覽全文，藉標示詞Although（雖然）猜測前後句應呈現對比的意義，取樣前句的動詞片語represents the sunset of the Renaissance（代表文藝復興時期的衰落）。
預測	後句的空格內應填入表示對比或反義的詞語。represents the sunset of the Renaissance是表「負向」的動詞片語，答案應選具有正向的動詞片語possessed a _____ .，預測選項Ⓑ virtuosity（精湛技藝）為可能答案。這句話的意思是貝尼尼雖然生活在文藝復興衰弱期，但其精湛技藝可以和文藝復興三傑中的李奧納多或米開朗基羅相媲美。
檢驗	將 Ⓑ 選項填入空格中檢驗句意。
確認	瀏覽上下句，整體句意連貫，確認答案為 Ⓑ，正確答案就在題目上。

5. In fact, in contemporary society the transition **from** pleasant child **to** dramatically _____ teenager, with an ego like a hedgehog that raises its spikes at the slightest touch, tends to happen earlier and earlier.

   Ⓐ stringent　　Ⓑ sprawling　　Ⓒ truculent　　Ⓓ sporadic

中譯	事實上，在當今社會，從和氣可愛的孩童轉變為明顯兇蠻的青少年，往往會越來越早發生，他們的自大就像在稍微觸碰時就豎起尖刺的刺一樣。 Ⓐ 嚴格的；緊縮的　　Ⓑ 蔓延的；雜亂無序伸展的 Ⓒ 粗暴的；野蠻的　　Ⓓ 偶爾發生的；斷斷續續的
取樣	瀏覽全文，藉標示詞from A to B（從……到……）猜測to的前後A、B應呈現對比或反義的意義，取樣pleasant (child)（和氣可愛的孩童）。
預測	後句的空格內應填入表示對比pleasant (child) 的字詞，pleasant是表示「正向」語意的形容詞，答案應選具有「負向」語意的形容詞，預測選項 Ⓒ truculent（兇蠻的）為可能答案。
檢驗	將 Ⓒ 選項填入空格中檢驗句意。
確認	瀏覽上下句，整體句意連貫，確認答案為 Ⓒ，正確答案就在題目上。

6. John's neighbors never really liked him **even though** plaques and medals proved he had done very _____ work in the community.

Ⓐ laudable　　Ⓑ mawkish　　Ⓒ implacable　　Ⓓ ephemeral

中譯	雖然匾額和獎牌已證明約翰在社區做過非常值得稱讚的工作，但鄰居們從未真正喜歡過他。 Ⓐ 應受讚揚的；值得讚美的　Ⓑ 令人作嘔的；傷感的 Ⓒ 毫不留情的；難和解的　　Ⓓ 短暫的；瞬息的
取樣	瀏覽全文，藉標示詞 even though（即使）猜測前後兩句應呈現對比的意義，取樣否定詞never（從未）、動詞liked（喜歡）。
預測	空格內應填入表示對比never liked的字詞，never liked具有「負向」含義，前句表達「負向」含義，後句應具有「正向」含義，空格需填入和「liked（喜歡）」有關的形容詞，預測選項 Ⓐ laudable（應受讚揚的；值得讚美的）為可能答案。

檢驗	將 Ⓐ 選項填入空格中檢驗句意。
確認	瀏覽上下句，整體句意連貫，確認答案為 Ⓐ，正確答案就在題目上。

7. **For all** the artistic wonders it has preserved, the Holy Mountain is not a museum, and the idea of playing host to sightseers is ＿＿＿＿＿＿ to the monks.

   Ⓐ anarchy　　Ⓑ anathema　　Ⓒ anesthesia　　Ⓓ anatomy

中譯	儘管聖山保存了藝術奇蹟，但它並不是一座博物館，接待參觀者成了僧侶們<u>極為厭惡的想法</u>。 Ⓐ 無政府狀態；混亂　Ⓑ 極令人厭惡之事物；可惡的想法 Ⓒ 麻木、知覺喪失　　　Ⓓ （動植物的）結構、解剖
詞彙解說	anathema本指「獻祭品」，源自古希臘複合動詞anatithénai，意思是「放置在（廟宇）上級處」，因此產生「把某物獻給神祇」的意思，由希臘文前綴 ana-（向上）和動詞 tithénai（放置）組合而成。起初，anathema 意思較廣泛，意思是「任何為宗教目的奉獻的東西」，但這個詞後來逐漸產生了負面意涵，變成了「奉獻給邪靈的東西」的意思。傳入拉丁文後更貶低為「詛咒」或「被詛咒者」的意思，甚至有「遭羅馬天主教開除教籍的人」及「遭逐出教會者」的意思。現代英語中的 anathema 保留了這種強烈的否定和憎惡的意味，通常用來描述被視為極端不受歡迎或可憎的事物、觀點或人物。
取樣	瀏覽全文，藉標示詞 for all（儘管）猜測第一個逗點前後應呈現對比或反義的意義，取樣名詞片語artistic wonders（藝術奇蹟）。此外，取樣否定詞not（不是）和名詞片語a museum（博物館）。
預測	空格內應填入表示對比artistic wonders的字詞，artistic wonders 具有「正向」含義，前面由介系詞片語for all引導的片語應具有「正向」含義，因此後面句子的空格中需填入一個具有「負向」含義的字，預測選項 Ⓑ anathema（可憎的事物；可惡的想法）為可能答案。此外，句中提到聖山並非一座博物館，用

	and接著說僧侶們厭惡接待參觀者的想法，為什麼？因平日僧侶們的職責並非擔任博物館解說員，現在一想到要接待川流不息參訪artistic wonders的遊客，難免會產生厭惡感。
檢驗	將 Ⓑ 選項填入空格中檢驗句意。
確認	瀏覽上下句，整體句意連貫，確認答案為 Ⓑ，正確答案就在題目上。

8. **Whereas** there are recent reports of declines in movie violence and fewer portrayals of violence as _____, media portraits of crime greatly overemphasize individual acts of violence.

Ⓐ graphic　　Ⓑ annexed　　Ⓒ negative　　Ⓓ damaging

中譯	儘管最近有報導稱電影暴力有所減少，較少繪聲繪色地描述暴力，但媒體對犯罪的描繪卻極度過分強調個人的暴力行為。 Ⓐ 生動的、栩栩如生的　　Ⓑ 被併吞的；附加的 Ⓒ 否定的；消極的　　　　Ⓓ 造成破壞的；有害的
取樣	瀏覽全文，藉標示詞Whereas（然而、可是、儘管）猜測前後兩句應呈現對比或反義的意義，取樣動詞片語greatly overemphasize individual acts of violence（極度過分強調個人的暴力行為）。此外，也取樣前句具有否定意味的fewer（較少）。
預測	空格內應填入表示對比greatly overemphasize individual acts of violence的字詞，overemphasize individual acts of violence具有「負向」含義，後句表達「負向」含義，前句應具有「正向」含義，預測選項 Ⓐ graphic（生動的、栩栩如生的）為可能答案，較少繪聲繪色地描述暴力具有「正向」含義。
檢驗	將 Ⓐ 選項填入空格中檢驗句意。
確認	瀏覽上下句，整體句意連貫，確認答案為 Ⓐ，正確答案就在題目上。

9. Old as the continents are, they are apparently **not** _____ features of the earth **but rather** secondary features that have formed and evolved during the earth's lifetime.

   Ⓐ incongruous   Ⓑ kaleidoscopic   Ⓒ frolicsome   Ⓓ primordial

中譯	儘管大陸很古老，但它們顯然不是地球的原始特徵，而是在地球的生命週期中形成，演變而來的次要特徵。 Ⓐ 不合適的；不相稱的 Ⓑ 像萬花筒似的（風景、顏色等）；千變萬化的 Ⓒ 嬉戲的；作樂的　　Ⓓ 原生的；原始的；最初的
取樣	瀏覽全文，藉標示詞 not A but rather B（不是……而是）猜測 but rather前後A、B應呈現對比的意義，取樣形容詞secondary（次要的）。此外，A、B要有對稱的結構adj.+N。
預測	空格內應填入表示對比secondary的字詞，預測選項Ⓓ primordial（原生的；原始的）為可能答案。注意，Old as (=though) the continents are, 中的as意思為「儘管」、「雖然」、「即使」，等同於Although the continents are old, 為讓讀者清楚了解這種將形容詞／副詞／（無冠詞的）名詞置於as／though前面的倒裝用法，現舉若干句子說明如下： 1. 形容詞 + as/though + 從屬子句 **Tired as/though** he was, he still went to the gym. (=Although he was tired, ...) 儘管他很累，但還是去了健身房。 **Poor as/though** she was, she was always very happy. (=Although she was poor, ...) 雖然他很窮，但總是很高興。 　**比較**　Poor as he was, it is not surprising that he should have stolen the bread.（因為他很窮，難怪他偷了麵包。）句中的as表示「因為」，不可和表示「雖然」、「儘管」的as混為一談。 　**備註**　也有人認為**形容詞 + as + 從屬子句**這個句型是**As + 形容詞 + as + 從屬子句**的省略，例如：**Tired as** he was, he still went to the gym. 是**As tired as** he was, he still went to the gym. 的省略。Michael Swan在*Practical Englih Usage*一書中也提到

預測	在美國英語中，常用as...as，請參看書中例子：**As cold as** it was, we went out. (儘管天氣很冷，我們還是出去了。) 2. **副詞 + as/though + 從屬子句** **Highly as/though** they were educated, they were still unable to get a job. (=Although they were highly educated, ...) 儘管他們受過高等教育，但仍然找不到工作。 **Richly as/though** they were rewarded, they were still not satisfied. (=Although they were richly rewarded, ...) 儘管他們得到了豐厚的回報，但仍然不滿足。 **Beautifully as/though** she was dressed, she still felt insecure. (=Although she was beautifully dressed, ...) 儘管她穿著打扮得很漂亮，但仍然感到沒有自信。 3. **（無冠詞的）名詞 + though + 從屬子句** **Child though** she was, she was remarkably wise. (=Although she was a child, ...) 她雖然是個孩子，但非常聰明。 **Novice though** he was, he played the piano masterfully. (=Although he was a novice, ...) 他雖然是個新手，但彈鋼琴彈得非常嫻熟。 **備註** Michael Swan在*Practical Englih Usage*一書中提到though可以用在名詞之後，而as不行。
檢驗	將 ❶ 選項填入空格中檢驗句意。
確認	瀏覽上下句，整體句意連貫，確認答案為 ❶，正確答案就在題目上。

10. Very often, the formation of a barren desert is considered to be caused by a lack of rainfall. **Nevertheless**, low _____ alone does **not necessarily** make an area a desert.

   Ⓐ prescription   Ⓑ predicament   Ⓒ predilection   Ⓓ precipitation

中譯	人們常常認為荒漠的形成是缺乏降雨造成的。然而，單單<u>低降水量</u>並不一定會使一個地區成為沙漠。 Ⓐ 處方；藥方　Ⓑ 尷尬的處境；困境 Ⓒ 喜愛；偏愛　Ⓓ 雨、雪（量）；（雨、雪等的）降落
取樣	瀏覽全文，藉標示詞Nevertheless（然而）猜測前後兩句應呈現對照的意義，取樣第一句中表「因」的名詞片語a lack of rainfall（缺乏降雨）。
預測	Nevertheless後面的句子用以反駁前句，前句的論述是：人們認為荒漠的形成是缺乏降雨造成的，後句應提出缺乏降雨未必（not necessarily）造成荒漠來反駁前句。後一句中已經出現表示「部分否定」的not necessarily（不一定、未必）來否定這個論點，空格應填入和a lack of rainfall語意相近的字詞，因為題目中已經出現關鍵形容詞low（低的），對應前一句的lack（缺乏），因此只需選一個和rainfall（降雨量）同義的字，預測選項 Ⓓ precipitation（降水、降水量）為可能答案。
檢驗	將 Ⓓ 選項填入空格中檢驗句意。
確認	瀏覽上下句，整體句意連貫，確認答案為 Ⓓ，正確答案就在題目上。

11. **Even if** you move abroad, it does not ＿＿＿＿＿＿ you from the obligation of paying the property tax. So you always have to pay like you do now.

　　Ⓐ absolve　Ⓑ amend　Ⓒ discredit　Ⓓ divert

中譯	即使你移居國外，也不能<u>免除</u>你繳納房地產稅的義務。所以你得像現在一樣繳納稅款。 Ⓐ 免除（責任、義務等）；赦免（罪惡） Ⓑ 修正、修訂（法律、文件、聲明等） Ⓒ 不信任；懷疑　Ⓓ 使轉向；使分心
取樣	瀏覽全文，藉標示詞 Even if（即使）猜測前後兩句應呈現對比的意義，取樣動詞片語move abroad（移居國外）及否定詞not（不）。此外，藉標示詞so（所以）猜測前後應呈現因果關係，

取樣	取樣動詞片語always have to pay like you do now（還是得像現在一樣繳納稅款）。
預測	空格內應填入表示對比move abroad的字詞，那要填什麼呢？依據上下文情境和實際課稅狀況判斷，知道有些國家的稅制是即便你移居國外，仍然需要你付原國籍擁有房地產的房地產稅，而非對居住地課稅，因為句中已有否定詞not，預測選項 Ⓐ absolve（免除……的責任）為可能答案，表示不能免除繳納房地產稅的義務。此外，從so後面所接表示「結果」的句子中的always have to pay like you do now判斷，可以得知表「原因」的前句應該也要傳遞「還是得像現在一樣繳納」這個「結果」的概念，更可以印證選項 Ⓐ absolve（免除……的責任）是正解。注意，absolve +人+ from + 事 的意思是「免除、解除人的（義務、責任等）」，例如： absolve a person from an obligation（免除某人的義務）。
檢驗	將 Ⓐ 選項填入空格中檢驗句意。
確認	瀏覽上下句，整體句意連貫，確認答案為 Ⓐ，正確答案就在題目上。

12. **Although** eighteenth-century English society as a whole did not encourage learning for its own sake in women, **nonetheless** it illogically _____ women's sad lack of education.

   Ⓐ brooked   Ⓑ vaunted   Ⓒ palliated   Ⓓ decried

中譯	儘管18世紀的英國社會整體上並不鼓勵女性為學習而學習，但仍然不合常理地批評女性教育的嚴重不足。 Ⓐ 容忍（用於否定結構）　　Ⓑ 自誇、炫耀 Ⓒ 減輕、緩和（疾病或不適） Ⓓ （公開）譴責；（強烈）批評
取樣	瀏覽全文，藉標示詞Although（雖然）、nonetheless（然而）猜測前後兩句應呈現對比的意義，取樣副詞子句中的否定詞 not（不）和動詞片語encourage learning for its own sake in women（鼓勵女性為學習而學習）。

預測	空格內應填入表示對比not encourage learning for its own sake in women的字詞，那要填什麼呢？依據常理推斷，當一個社會整體上不鼓勵女性為學習而學習，那這個社會對於女性教育的嚴重不足應不會批評或譴責，然而本題開頭用了Although來表示和預期中的不同，答案應選和批評相關具有「負向」含義的動詞，預測選項 **D** decried（（公開）譴責；（強烈）批評）為可能答案。
檢驗	將 **D** 選項填入空格中檢驗句意。
確認	瀏覽上下句，整體句意連貫，確認答案為 **D**，正確答案就在題目上。

13. The president who is proud of his _____ background has now **ironically** accumulated a huge amount of wealth for his family and relatives.

A monotheistic　　**B** polygamous　　**C** proletarian　　**D** Socratic

中譯	這位以其<u>無產階級</u>出身為傲的總統，如今為他的家人和親戚積累了巨額財富，相當諷刺。 **A** 一神教的、一神論的 **B** 多配偶的、一夫多妻（一妻多夫）的 **C** 無產階級的；普羅階級的　　**D** 蘇格拉底（哲學）的
取樣	瀏覽全文，藉標示詞ironically（諷刺地）猜測前後應呈現對比的意義，取樣動詞片語accumulated a huge amount of wealth（積累了巨額財富）。
預測	空格內應填入表示對比accumulated a huge amount of wealth的字詞，這句話描繪了這位總統的無產/有產矛盾之處，無產階級出身卻累積巨大財富，預測選項 **C** proletariat（無產階級）為可能答案。
檢驗	將 **C** 選項填入空格中檢驗句意。
確認	瀏覽上下句，整體句意連貫，確認答案為 **C**，正確答案就在題目上。值得一提的是，原題 **C** 選項proletariat為名詞，而其他三個選項為形容詞，以測驗與評量的觀點來看，明顯暗示 **C** 選項

| 確認 | proletariat為正解，會影響考試的信效度，因此作者建議將該選項修改為形容詞proletarian。此外，proletarian background比proletariat background的搭配更為常見。 |

14. Doctors said that the conventional medicine can only _____ the condition, **but** it cannot cure them for good.

Ⓐ palliate　　Ⓑ captivate　　Ⓒ extirpate　　Ⓓ recapitulate

中譯	醫生說，傳統醫學只能緩解病情，無法徹底治癒。 Ⓐ（暫時）減輕（疾病等）；緩和（痛苦）等 Ⓑ 使（人）著迷、使……迷惑 Ⓒ 消滅、根除　　Ⓓ 重述；概括
取樣	瀏覽全文，藉標示詞but（但）猜測前後兩句應呈現對比的意義，取樣後句中的動詞only（只）、否定詞not（無法）和動詞片語cure them for good（徹底治癒病情）。for good意思是「永久地」（forever; permanently），修飾動詞cure。
預測	空格內應填入表示對比not cure them for good（永久地）的字詞，正確答案應該跟「無法徹底治癒」有關，預測選項 Ⓐ palliate（暫時減輕疾病等）為可能答案。傳統醫學無法徹底治癒病情，只能舒緩病情。
檢驗	將 Ⓐ 選項填入空格中檢驗句意。
確認	瀏覽上下句，整體句意連貫，確認答案為 Ⓐ，正確答案就在題目上。

15. **Initially** only the carpeting outside the restroom was _____ by water from burst pipe; **eventually** the entire hallway flooded.

Ⓐ confined　　Ⓑ scuttled　　Ⓒ cleansed　　Ⓓ drenched

| 中譯 | 一開始只有洗手間外面的地毯被爆裂水管的水淋濕了，最終整個走廊都淹水了。
Ⓐ 限制；監禁　　Ⓑ 破壞、阻止
Ⓒ 清潔（皮膚）　　Ⓓ 浸透、浸泡、淋透 |

取樣	drench的意思是「浸透」、「浸泡」、「淋透」。/d/ 與注音符號ㄉ唸音相似，都是「水滴」的擬聲音，因此與水或水滴相關的詞常以dr-為首，例如：drain（v.排水；n.排水管、排水道）、drown (v.淹死；浸濕)。（欲知更多dr-語音表義的例子，請參考《音義聯想單字記憶法》p.180。）
預測	前句的空格內應填入表示對比flooded（淹水）的字詞，依常理推斷，水管破裂，一開始水可能只會弄濕一些東西，例如地毯，但如果不處理，最後會把整個（entire）走廊浸泡在水中，預測選項 **D** drenched（被浸泡）為可能答案。
檢驗	將 **D** 選項填入空格中檢驗句意。
確認	瀏覽上下句，整體句意連貫，確認答案為 **D**，正確答案就在題目上。

16. **Instead of** giving us any real insight into the controversial issue, the speaker just threw ＿＿＿＿＿＿ at the attendees for the entire two hours. It was indeed a boring speech.

A harangues　　**B** prerogatives　　**C** sycophants　　**D** conundrums

中譯	這位講者並沒有就這個爭議性問題給我們任何真知灼見，只是在整個兩個小時裡對與會者發表長篇的激烈批評。確實是一個無聊的演講。 **A**（對公眾集會作的）大聲疾呼的長篇演說、長篇的高談闊論 **B** 特權；優先權　　**C** 阿諛奉承的人；諂媚者 **D** 令人迷惑的難題；複雜難解的問題
取樣	瀏覽全文，藉標示詞 Instead of（代替、而不是）猜測逗點前後應呈現對比的意義，取樣動名詞片語giving us any real insight（給我們任何真知灼見）。
預測	空格內應填入表示對比giving us any real insight的字詞。giving us any real insight具有「正向」含義，而後半的句子表達「負向」含義，因此空格中需填入一個跟「缺乏真知灼見」有關，且具有「負向」含義的字，預測選項 **A** harangues（（對公眾集會作的）大聲疾呼之長篇演說、長篇之高談闊論）為可能答案。

檢驗	將 Ⓐ 選項填入空格中檢驗句意。
確認	瀏覽上下句，整體句意連貫，確認答案為 Ⓐ，正確答案就在題目上。

17. The principal prefers not to _____ student misbehavior publicly; **instead**, she asks the troublemakers to go to her office and talks to them about their problems.

　　Ⓐ validate　　Ⓑ repudiate　　Ⓒ modulate　　Ⓓ castigate

中譯	校長傾向不公開嚴懲學生行為不端；但她卻會要求鬧事者去她的辦公室，並與他們談論問題。 Ⓐ 證實；確認　Ⓑ 拒絕（要求等）；不接受 Ⓒ 調節（嗓音的大小、強弱、高低等） Ⓓ 對……實施嚴厲的懲罰；嚴厲批評
取樣	瀏覽全文，藉標示詞 instead（相反地）猜測前後兩句應呈現對比的意義，取樣後句的動詞片語asks the troublemakers to go to her office（要求鬧事者去她的辦公室）和talks to them about their problems（與他們談論問題）。此外，也取樣前句的否定詞not（不）。
預測	空格內應填入表示輕重程度的對比asks the troublemakers to go to her office和talks to them about their problems的字詞，go to her office和talks to them about their problems雖是懲罰，但屬較輕的懲罰，因此前句空格應填重懲，預測選項 Ⓓ castigate（對……實施嚴厲的懲罰；嚴厲批評）為可能答案。
檢驗	將 Ⓓ 選項填入空格中檢驗句意。句意是不（not）採取嚴懲，而採取輕懲。
確認	瀏覽上下句，整體句意連貫，確認答案為 Ⓓ，正確答案就在題目上。

18. The speaker declared that the focal point of his speech would be on extensive global issues **rather than** on _____ issues.

Ⓐ parochial　Ⓑ perennial　Ⓒ disdainful　Ⓓ contagious

中譯	演講者宣稱他的演講焦點將放在廣泛的全球議題上，而非<u>地方性議題</u>。 Ⓐ 地方性的；教區的　Ⓑ 四季不斷的；持續的 Ⓒ 輕視的；鄙視的　　Ⓓ （疾病）接觸傳染的
取樣	瀏覽全文，藉標示詞rather than（而非）猜測前後應呈現對比或反義的意義，取樣形容詞extensive global（廣泛的全球的）。
預測	空格內應填入表示對比或反義extensive global的字詞，預測選項 Ⓐ parochial（教區的；地方性的）為可能答案。global ≠ parochial。
檢驗	將 Ⓐ 選項填入空格中檢驗句意。
確認	瀏覽上下句，整體句意連貫，確認答案為 Ⓐ，正確答案就在題目上。

19. In spite of the mayor's _____ denial that he was involved in the illegal insider trading, many of the residents still thought that he had committed a crime.

Ⓐ venial　Ⓑ vapid　Ⓒ vehement　Ⓓ variegated

中譯	儘管市長<u>激烈</u>否認自己涉及非法內線交易，許多居民仍然認為他犯了罪。 Ⓐ 可原諒的；（過失）輕微的　Ⓑ 乏味的；枯燥的 Ⓒ 激情的、激烈的　　　　　　Ⓓ 斑駁的；雜色的
取樣	瀏覽全文，藉標示詞In spite of（儘管）猜測前後句應呈現對比的意義，取樣後面的動詞片語still thought that he had committed a crime（居民仍然認為他犯了罪）。
預測	空格內應填入表示對比still thought that he had committed a crime的字詞，居民認為市長犯了罪，但市長本人矢口否認涉

58　Chapter 2　認識對比、反義結構：BUT 型

預測	案，預測選項 **C** vehement（（感情）強烈的、激烈的）為可能答案。注意，是指「強烈的」、「激烈的」，通常用於描述情感或言語，vehement denial即「激烈否認」。
檢驗	將 **C** 選項填入空格中檢驗句意。
確認	瀏覽上下句，整體句意連貫，確認答案為 **C**，正確答案就在題目上。

20. The new movie sequel immediately became divisive, with some praising the film's intense fight choreography, **while** others ＿＿＿＿ the director for changing major facets of the main character.

Ⓐ nullified   **Ⓑ** lamented   **Ⓒ** lambasted   **Ⓓ** perforate

中譯	這部新電影的續集一推出立即引起爭議，因有些人讚揚電影激烈的打鬥動作編排，而另一些人則痛批導演改變主角的重要面。 Ⓐ 使失去法律效力；廢止　Ⓑ 對……感到悲痛；痛惜 Ⓒ 猛烈抨擊；嚴厲申斥　Ⓓ 打孔；穿孔
取樣	瀏覽全文，藉標示詞while（（對比兩件事物）……而，……然而）猜測前後兩句應呈現對比或反義的意義，取樣介系詞片語中的現在分詞praising（讚揚；稱讚）。
預測	空格內應填入表示praising反義的字詞，預測選項 **C** lambasted（猛烈抨擊；嚴厲申斥）為可能答案。
檢驗	將 **C** 選項填入空格中檢驗句意。
確認	瀏覽上下句，整體句意連貫，確認答案為 **C**，正確答案就在題目上。

21. Even though her statement sounded like a perfectly ＿＿＿＿ remark, her husband still thought she slighted him.

Ⓐ dilapidated   **Ⓑ** inviable   **Ⓒ** regressive   **Ⓓ** innocuous

中譯	儘管她的說法聽起來像是一句完全無惡意的話，她的丈夫仍然認為她輕視了他。 Ⓐ 破舊的；破爛的　Ⓑ 不能生存的 Ⓒ 退化的；倒退的　Ⓓ 無惡意的；無害的
取樣	瀏覽全文，藉標示詞 Even though（儘管）猜測前後兩句應呈現對比的意義，取樣後句的動詞slighted（輕視、蔑視、侮辱）。
預測	空格內應填入表示對比slighted的字詞，slighted具有「負向」含義，前句應表達「正向」含義，預測選項 Ⓓ innocuous（無惡意的；無害的）為可能答案，innocuous remark即「無惡意的話」。
檢驗	將 Ⓓ 選項填入空格中檢驗句意。
確認	瀏覽上下句，整體句意連貫，確認答案為 Ⓓ，正確答案就在題目上。

22. The labor union and the company's management, **despite** their long history of unfailingly acerbic disagreement on nearly every issue, have **nevertheless** reached an **unexpectedly** ＿＿＿＿, **albeit** still tentative, agreement on next year's contract.

Ⓐ swift　Ⓑ onerous　Ⓒ hesitant　Ⓓ reluctant

中譯	工會和公司管理部門雖然幾乎在每個問題上都有的確很尖銳的紛歧已有一段很長的歷史，但他們仍然出乎意料地迅速達成了明年合約的暫時協議。 Ⓐ 迅速的、即時的　Ⓑ 費力的；艱鉅的 Ⓒ 猶豫的；躊躇的　Ⓓ 不情願的；勉強的
取樣	瀏覽全文，藉標示詞despite（儘管）、nevertheless（然而）、unexpectedly（出人意料地）猜測前後兩句應呈現對比的意義，取樣名詞片語long history of unfailingly acerbic disagreement（長期的尖銳紛歧）。
預測	空格內應填入表示對比long history of unfailingly acerbic

預測	disagreement的字詞，依常理推斷，要化解長期的尖銳紛歧耗時費工，很難迅速達成任何協議，但工會和公司管理部門卻能迅速達成暫時協議，預測選項 Ⓐ swift（迅速的）為可能答案。
檢驗	將 Ⓐ 選項填入空格中檢驗句意。
確認	瀏覽上下句，整體句意連貫，確認答案為 Ⓐ，正確答案就在題目上。

23. **Despite** his efforts to reconcile with his estranged cousin, the latter continued to make ＿＿＿＿ remarks about him during family gatherings.

Ⓐ derogatory　　Ⓑ gregarious　　Ⓒ laudable　　Ⓓ pedagogical
Ⓔ translucent

中譯	他雖然努力與疏遠的表親和解，但在家庭聚會期間，後者仍然繼續對他發表誹謗的言辭。 Ⓐ 貶低的；誹謗的　　　　　Ⓑ 社交的；合群的 Ⓒ 應受讚揚的；值得讚美的　Ⓓ 教育學的；教學的 Ⓔ 半透明的
取樣	瀏覽全文，藉標示詞Despite（儘管；然而）猜測前後應呈現對比的意義，取樣動詞片語reconcile with his estranged cousin（與疏遠的表親和解）。
預測	空格內應填入表示對比reconcile with his estranged cousin的字詞，與疏遠的表親和解具有「正面」含義，但結果不如人願，答案應具有「負面」含義，預測選項 Ⓐ derogatory（貶低的；誹謗的）為可能答案。derogatory remark即「誹謗的言辭」。
檢驗	將 Ⓐ 選項填入空格中檢驗句意。
確認	瀏覽上下句，整體句意連貫，確認答案為 Ⓐ，正確答案就在題目上。

24. The problems that fester in our healthcare system are not _____. **Quite on the contrary**, they constitute major challenges in today's hospitals.

Ⓐ perpendicular　　Ⓑ eccentric　　Ⓒ holistic
Ⓓ epicenter　　Ⓔ peripheral

中譯	我們醫療系統中愈益煩惱的問題並非<u>膚淺的</u>。恰恰相反，它們構成了當今醫院面臨的主要挑戰。 Ⓐ 垂直的；成直角的　　Ⓑ 古怪的；異乎尋常的 Ⓒ 整體的；全面的　　Ⓓ （地震的）震央 Ⓔ 次要的；邊緣的；膚淺的
取樣	瀏覽全文，藉標示詞Quite on the contrary（恰恰相反）猜測前後句應呈現對比的意義，取樣後句的動詞片語constitute major challenges（構成主要挑戰）具有「負面」含意，但前句有否定詞not，因此空格中需填入一個具有「負面」含意的詞語，「負負得正」才能使前句表達「正面」的含意。
預測	後句的空格內應填入表示對比major (challenges)的字詞，預測選項 Ⓔ peripheral（膚淺的）為可能答案。
檢驗	將 Ⓔ 選項填入空格中檢驗句意。
確認	瀏覽上下句，整體句意連貫，確認答案為 Ⓔ，正確答案就在題目上。

25. For decades, as you probably know, researchers have found that when you tell patients that you're giving them medicine, many report that their symptoms are _____, **even if** they're only taking sugar pills.

Ⓐ intoxicated　　Ⓑ conglomerated　　Ⓒ alleviated　　Ⓓ equivocated

中譯	正如你可能知道的，幾十年來，研究人員發現，你告訴患者你正給他們藥物時，即使他們只是服用糖丸，許多人報告他們的症狀得到了<u>緩解</u>。 Ⓐ 使喝醉；使陶醉　　Ⓑ 結聚成一團 Ⓒ 緩解；減輕痛苦　　Ⓓ 含糊其詞；用雙關語

取樣	瀏覽全文，藉標示詞 even if（即使）猜測前後句應呈現對比的意義，取樣動詞片語 only taking sugar pills（只是服用糖丸）。
預測	後句的空格內應填入表示對比 only taking sugar pills 的字詞，按常理推論 only taking sugar pills 沒有治療的效果，無法讓症狀緩和，具有「負面」含意，但只要患者不知情，以為這藥丸是藥物，症狀還是會得到舒緩，具有「正面」含意，預測選項 ⓒ alleviated（緩解）為可能答案。
檢驗	將 ⓒ 選項填入空格中檢驗句意。
確認	瀏覽上下句，整體句意連貫，確認答案為 ⓒ，正確答案就在題目上。

實戰練習

1. "July and August are off-season months for tourism in southern Baja, so it could be an affordable time to visit. _____, the heat can be oppressive, and it's hurricane season," explained Uncle Neil.

   Ⓐ Meanwhile   **Ⓑ On the other hand**   Ⓒ In other words
   Ⓓ Furthermore

2. _____ companions usually disappear by the time children head off to school, **but** if one child still has a pretend friend by grade one or two, evaluate whether it's preventing him from socializing normally.

   Ⓐ Imaginative   Ⓑ Imaginary   Ⓒ Insane   Ⓓ Invective

3. **In spite of** its potential danger, many people believe that nuclear energy is a cleaner and more _____ source of energy which will not be used up in a short time.

   Ⓐ fastidious   Ⓑ synthetic   Ⓒ inexhaustible   Ⓓ lunatic

4. **Apart from** the _____ and the pressure of being watched under a gun, the female hostage seemed in good spirits.

   A decline **B** proliferation **C** seclusion **D** dexterity

5. **Despite** the subtle changes in the design, differences between the two generations of the smartphone was immediately _____ to even the most casual observer, as the newer model boasted a larger screen, slimmer profile, and upgraded camera system.

   A discernible **B** infallible **C** accessible **D** illegible

6. After years of the English language being _____ by text messages and hashtags, dictionaries have made a **surprising** comeback in the United States.

   A promoted **B** elevated **C** degraded **D** offended

7. This traveling experience was rated mediocre. The food was good **but**, **unfortunately**, we found the rest of the itinerary distinctly _____.

   A veracious **B** succinct **C** underwhelming **D** pungent

8. Afraid of being punished, Jeff gave his teacher a(n) _____ reason for his absence, saying that he had a fever this morning, **while** the fact was that he overslept and failed to catch the bus to school.

   A embedded **B** ostensible **C** lucrative **D** unsettling

9. The Winged Victory statue lacks a head, _____ it is considered one of the world's most beautiful sculptures.

   A nevertheless **B** still **C** despite **D** **yet** **E** therefore

10. A new study suggests that there seems to be a limit to human lifespan. **However**, the results, based on demographic data, are **far from** _____ and must be interpreted carefully.

Ⓐ suggestive   Ⓑ conclusive   Ⓒ ambiguous   Ⓓ doubtful

11. With this faith in racial justice, we'll be able to **transform** this _____ discord of our nation **into** a beautiful symphony of brotherhood.

Ⓐ jangling   Ⓑ dolce   Ⓒ congruous   Ⓓ presumptive

12. Whereas social support might have helped female migrant workers to _____ the effects of migrant stress on their mental health, no such effect was found among the male migrant workers.

Ⓐ counteract   Ⓑ deliver   Ⓒ highlight   Ⓓ integrate

解答

1. Ⓑ   2. Ⓑ   3. Ⓒ   4. Ⓒ   5. Ⓐ   6. Ⓒ   7. Ⓒ   8. Ⓑ   9. Ⓓ   10. Ⓑ
11. Ⓐ   12. Ⓐ

Chapter 3

認識因果關係：

BECAUSE 型

題型解說

Because 型【因果關係（cause and effect）】

表「因果關係」最常見的方式是用從屬連接詞，以 because 的語氣最強，其次是 since、as。

A as、since、because

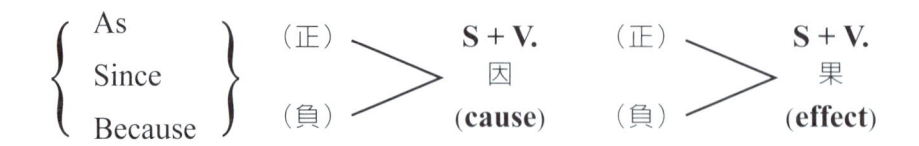

$$\begin{Bmatrix} As \\ Since \\ Because \end{Bmatrix} \begin{matrix}（正）\\（負）\end{matrix} > \underset{(cause)}{\underset{因}{S + V.}} \begin{matrix}（正）\\（負）\end{matrix} > \underset{(effect)}{\underset{果}{S + V.}}$$

這三個從屬連接詞表示「因為……所以……」的副詞子句，其因果語義強度依次遞減：because ＞ since ＞ as。

❶ <u>As</u> I'm leaving tomorrow, please come today.
因為明天我就要離開了，請今天過來吧。

▶ 重點在於主要子句，原因、理由很明顯，提出來只是附帶說明，常用於口語且用於句首

❷ The court's ruling set a dangerous ＿＿＿＿ for future cases, <u>as</u> it undermined the principle of equal protection under the law.
　Ⓐ precedent　**Ⓑ** accomplice　**Ⓒ** depiction　**Ⓓ** respondent
法院的裁決為未來的案件開創了危險的<u>先例</u>，因為它削弱了法律之前人人平等的保護原則。　　　　　　　　　　　　　　答案：A

❸ <u>Since</u> you insist, I will reconsider the matter.
既然你堅持，我就把此事再考慮一下。

▶ Since所說明的理由是附帶的，或對方已明白的，含有「既然……就」的意義，雖然語氣比較弱，但比as正式一點，使用時往往會把since的子句放在句首

❹ Since it is raining, you'd better take a taxi.
既然正在下雨，那你就最好搭計程車。

❺ Since Mr. Johnson was diagnosed with cancer, he made up his mind to _____ alcohol, tobacco, and even red meat.
Ⓐ importune　Ⓑ eschew　Ⓒ cavil　Ⓓ stigmatize
因為強生先生被診斷出患有癌症，他決心戒酒、戒菸，甚至戒紅肉。
答案：B

❻ I didn't go out because it rained.
因為下雨了，我沒有出門。

▶ 重點在於說明直接的原因或理由的副詞子句，因此because的子句通常置於主要子句後面，because之前可加not, only, simply, just, merely, mainly等副詞修飾。在回答Why...?問句時，只能用Because回答why的理由或原因

❼ Why do you like him?　你為什麼喜歡他？
Because he is kind.　因為他很親切。

❽ John teaches English not because he is good at it but because he is interested in it.
約翰教英語不是因為他擅長英語，而是因為他對英語有興趣。

❾ You must not eat too much merely because you are hungry.
你不可以只因為肚子餓而吃得太多。

▶ merely可用simply、only或just代之

題型解說　69

❿ 因為生病了，所以我沒去。

▶ 中文的「因為……所以……」不可譯為Because （或As）... so...

✗ Because I was sick, so I didn't go.

○ a) Because I was sick, I didn't go.

○ b) I was sick, so I didn't go.

說明

英文只能有一個主要子句（S+V），所以要遵守「主從分明」的原則。如果從屬連接詞 because 與對等連接詞 so 同時出現，就分不清楚誰主、誰從，所以英文裡不能同時把 because 和 so 用在同一個句子裡。同理類推，英文裡也不能有 although... but... 這樣的句子。

⓫ Most of the American poet Emily Dickinson's writings were published _____ because she was shy and didn't seek public attention during her lifetime.

Ⓐ postnatally　　Ⓑ predominantly

Ⓒ postoperatively　Ⓓ posthumously

美國詩人埃米莉·狄更生的大部分著作都是死後出版的，因為她生前很害羞，不追求公眾關注。

答案：D

Ⓑ 表「因果」關係最常用的對等連接詞，表「因」用for，表「果」用so。for表示說話者以自己的意見為原因，來推斷前述的結果，for之前常置以逗號（comma），所以不可置於句首。試比較：

❶ a) The river is so high because it has rained hard recently.
因為最近下雨下得很大，所以河水高漲。　▶ 直接的原因

b) It must have rained hard recently, for the river is so high.
最近一定下雨下得很大，因為河水高漲。　▶ 推斷的原因

70　Chapter 3 認識因果關係：BECAUSE 型

❷ a) John is loved by all of us <u>because</u> he is honest.
因為約翰誠實,所以他被大家所愛。 ▶ 直接的原因

b) John must be honest, <u>for</u> he is loved by all of us.
約翰想必誠實,因為他被大家所愛。 ▶ 推斷的原因

❸ When he began speaking in the auditorium, I was dumbfounded, <u>for</u> he had a very heavy speech impediment.
當他在禮堂開始演講時,我驚訝得說不出話來,因為他口吃嚴重。

對等連接詞 so(所以)連接兩個子句時,如例❹ b)和❺ b)前句是說明原因,後句是說明所產生的結果,例如:

❹ a) <u>As</u> it is late, I have to leave.
b) It is late, <u>so</u> I have to leave.
因為時間已晚,所以我必須離開。

❺ a) <u>As</u> we have a long way to go, we must start early.
b) We have a long way to go, <u>so</u> we must start early.
因為我們要走很長的路程,所以我們必須早動身。

❻ The chairlady grumbled, "We don't have time for a long meeting, so please keep your comments _____."
Ⓐ jejune　Ⓑ laconic　Ⓒ insouciant　Ⓓ strident
女主席抱怨道:「我們沒時間開長會,所以評論時請保持簡潔扼要。」　◀ 答案:B

❼ This weed was not _____ to the country, so when it was introduced by human migration, it caused an imbalance in the eco-system.
Ⓐ endemic　Ⓑ survival　Ⓒ pristine　Ⓓ impetuous
這種雜草不是這個國家的原生植物,因此在人類遷徙引入後,才導致了生態系統失衡。　◀ 答案:A

❸ 因果關係的結構，也可以用下列的連繫副詞或片語（conjunctive adverb or phrase）來表示：

因 (cause); {as a result, as a consequence, consequently, accordingly, therefore, hence, thus,} 果 (effect)

　　純連接詞（pure conjunction）如：so, for 等只能出現在第二句的句首，而連繫副詞（conjunctive adverbs）可以移位，可以出現在第二個句子的句首、句中或句尾。兩個句子之間，常用分號（semicolon）或句號（period）隔開。試比較下列的 so 與 therefore：

　　❶ 對等連接詞 so
　　　It was very hot, <u>so</u> we went swimming.
　　　因為天氣炎熱，我們都去游泳了。

　　❷ 連繫副詞 therefore
　　　a) It was very hot; <u>therefore</u>, we went swimming.
　　　b) It was very hot; we, <u>therefore</u>, went swimming.
　　　c) It was very hot; we went swimming, <u>therefore</u>.
　　　d) It was very hot. <u>Therefore</u>, we went swimming.
　　　e) It was very hot. We went swimming, <u>therefore</u>.

thus 是聯繫副詞，不能直接用來連接兩個句子，需透過連接詞 and 連接兩句：

❸ Some of the plants in the garden are more susceptible to frost damage than the others and thus need more care.
花園中有些植物比其他植物更易受霜凍損害，因此需要更多的照顧。

❹ The debate team found their opponents' arguments logical and consequently irrefutable.
　Ⓐ irritating　　Ⓑ challenging
　Ⓒ interesting　Ⓓ incontrovertible
辯論隊發現對手的論點是合乎邏輯的，因此無可辯駁。　答案：D

▶ 聯繫副詞 consequently

❺ These medical centers have discovered that acupuncture and moxibustion are effective in treating painful illnesses. Accordingly, a number of German health insurance companies that cover Chinese medicine costs have commissioned medical centers at several universities to make a thorough evaluation, on the basis of which they plan to expand their future coverage.
這些醫療中心發現針灸和艾灸對治療疼痛性疾病有效。因此，有些支付中醫治療費用的德國健康保險公司，已委託幾所大學的醫療中心詳細評估，以便在這個基礎上擴大未來的保險範圍。

▶ 聯繫副詞 accordingly

為求句子多樣化，不要每次都用對等連接詞，有時不妨使用連繫副詞，但在英文裡沒有表原因的連繫副詞與對等連接詞 for 相對應。

D 其他表「原因」的連接詞

❶ in that = in (the fact) that當連接詞使用，只能放主句後面。現代英語多用because來替代。

> 例

Men differ from brutes <u>in that</u> they can think and speak.
人不同於禽獸是因為人會思考與說話。

❷ seeing that(=because)當連接詞使用，意思是「鑒於；由於；因為」。

> 例

Seeing that Donnie Yen movie series has _____ my enthusiasm for learning Chinese kung-fu fighting, I can't wait to sign up for a training program to give it a try.

Ⓐ lubricated　**Ⓑ** indicted　**Ⓒ** rekindled　**Ⓓ** extinguished

由於甄子丹的系列電影重新點燃了我對學習中國功夫的熱情，我迫不及待要報名參加培訓課程，一試身手。　　　　　　　答案：C

E , so that （結果）所以

$$\underline{S + V}_{\text{因 (cause)}} \text{, so that } \underline{S + V}_{\text{果 (effect)}}$$

so that 用作連接詞，之前必須用逗號（,）與表原因的句子隔開。

❶ I couldn't get a taxi, <u>so that</u> I had to come here by bus.
我叫不到計程車，所以我得搭公車來這裡。

❷ Helen was tired, <u>so that</u> she went to bed early.
海倫累了，所以她很早就睡了。

> 說明

result in／result from 均為不及物動詞片語，不能用於被動態。但 attribute A to B (把 A 歸因於 B)，其動詞 attribute 是及物動詞，必須要有受詞，因此可用於被動語態。

例1
John ran fast <u>so that</u> he might catch the train. ▶表目的
約翰跑得快以便趕得上火車。

例2
One important purpose of the course is for the students to learn to make sound judgments <u>so that</u> they can differentiate between fact and opinion without difficulty.
這門課的一個重要目的是讓學生學會做出明智的判斷，(以便)使他們能夠毫無困難地區分事實和意見。

F so／such...that...　如此……以致於

$$S + \begin{Bmatrix} be \\ V \end{Bmatrix} so + \begin{Bmatrix} adj. \\ adv. \end{Bmatrix} + (a) + N（表原因）+ that\ S + V（表結果）.$$

S + be + such + (a) + (adj.) + N（表原因）+ that S + V（表結果）.

❶ John is such a good teacher that every student likes him.
約翰是如此好的一位老師，以致每個學生都喜歡他。

> 說明

such 為形容詞，修飾名詞 teacher；that 為從屬連接詞，引導一個表「結果」的副詞子句，修飾形容詞 such。因此若 such 省略，則 that 子句也就一起省略掉了，句子就恢復原狀：John is a good teacher.。

❷ He is such a ＿＿＿＿, contemptuous braggart that he takes delight in downplaying others.
　Ⓐ reverberant　Ⓑ vigilant　Ⓒ tempestuous　Ⓓ supercilious
　他是一個如此傲慢、看不起他人的吹牛大王，以貶低他人為樂。
　答案：D

❸ John is so good a teacher that every student likes him.
　約翰是如此好的一位老師，以致每個學生都喜歡他。

> **說明**
>
> so 是副詞，其後必須接形容詞或副詞，that 為從屬連接詞，引導一個表「結果」的副詞子句，修飾副詞 so。

❹ John ran so quickly that I couldn't catch him.
　約翰跑得如此快以致於我無法趕上。

❺ The speaker was so inspiring that everyone left the auditorium ＿＿＿＿ with a greater dedication to the cause.
　Ⓐ induced　Ⓑ insulated　Ⓒ imbued　Ⓓ impeached
　演講者如此鼓舞人心，以致於每個人離開禮堂都被感染對這個事業要有更強烈的奉獻精神。
　答案：C

Ⓖ 介系詞 with 引導表「因為」的副詞片語，如下例：

with + object + present participle (objective complement)

❶ With night coming on, we started for home.
　　　　Ｏ　　ＯＣ　　　　Ｖ
　夜晚將臨，我們便動身返家。

76　Chapter 3　認識因果關係：BECAUSE 型

❷ With pink cherry blossoms blooming everywhere, the valley _____ like a young bride under the bright spring sunshine.
　Ⓐ bounces　Ⓑ blushes　Ⓒ polishes　Ⓓ transfers
　因為粉紅色的櫻花遍地盛開，在明媚的春光下山谷就像年輕的新娘一樣紅了臉。
　答案：B

Ⓗ 因果關係的結構，也可以用下列動詞或動詞片語來表示：

(a) 因 (cause) { cause / lead to / contribute to / result in / bring about　|　give rise to / be the cause of / be responsible for / be the reason for } 果 (effect)

❶ Wars will cause/lead to/contribute to/result in/bring about very terrible disasters.
　戰爭會造成極為可怕的災難。

❷ The _____ effects of the medication caused Judy to drift off into a deep sleep, despite the noise and commotion around her.
　Ⓐ soporific　Ⓑ lenient　Ⓒ inclement　Ⓓ nefarious
　儘管周圍吵鬧喧囂，藥物的催眠作用使茱蒂慢慢陷入了深睡。
　答案：A

❸ Climate change has contributed to the shifting of Earth's axis of rotation, according to new research.
　根據新的研究，氣候變遷導致地球自轉軸偏移。

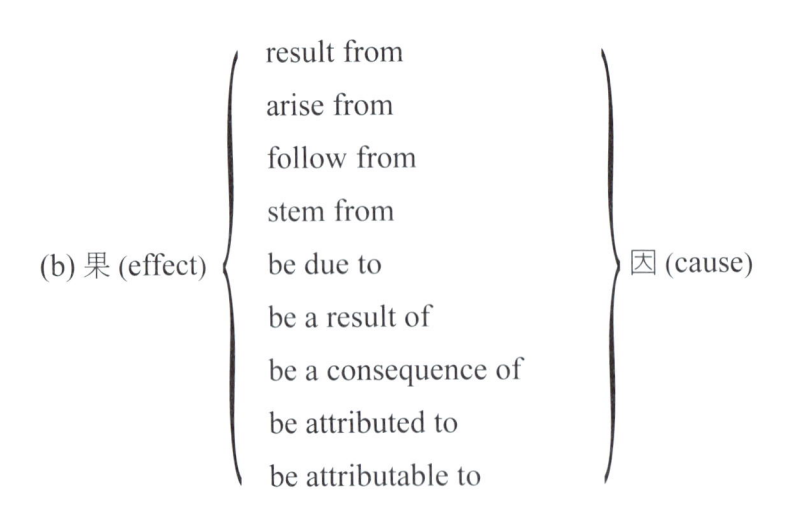

(b) 果 (effect)
$\begin{Bmatrix} \text{result from} \\ \text{arise from} \\ \text{follow from} \\ \text{stem from} \\ \text{be due to} \\ \text{be a result of} \\ \text{be a consequence of} \\ \text{be attributed to} \\ \text{be attributable to} \end{Bmatrix}$ 因 (cause)

現以 result in 與 result from 為例，說明如下：

❶ result in：產生或造成某種結果，句中主詞是「起因」，而 in 的受詞是「結果」。

例1

Eating too much often <u>results in</u> sickness.
過度飲食常導致疾病。

例2

Supporters of independence for Scotland have launched a grassroots campaign that may <u>result in</u> the ＿＿＿＿ of a 305-year-old union with England and the breakup of Britain.

Ⓐ demise　Ⓑ suffrage　Ⓒ deviancy　Ⓓ advent

支持蘇格蘭獨立的人士發起了群眾運動，可能導致與英格蘭的305年的聯盟終止，並導致英國分裂。　　　　　　　　　答案：A

❷ result from：由……引起；由……產生的，句中主詞是「結果」，而 from 的受詞是「起因」。

例1

Sickness often <u>results from</u> eating too much.
疾病常起因於過度飲食。

說明

result in／result from 均為不及物動詞片語，不能用於被動態。但 attribute A to B（把 A 歸因於 B），其動詞 attribute 是及物動詞，必須要有受詞，因此可用於被動語態。

✗ ❶ The damage <u>was resulted from</u> the fire.
✗ ❷ The fire <u>was resulted in</u> the damage.
　　這損害是由火災造成的。

例2

Although the processes of running a Nuclear Power plant generates no CO2, some CO2 emissions <u>arise from</u> the construction of the plant, the mining of the Uranium, the enrichment of the Uranium, its conversion into Nuclear Fuel, its final disposal and the final plant decommissioning.
雖然核電廠運轉的過程中不會產生二氧化碳，但建造核電廠、開採鈾礦、將鈾濃縮、將鈾轉化成核燃料、最終處置核廢料，核電廠最終退役過程會產生部分二氧化碳排放。

例3

America's pervasive gun culture <u>stems from</u> its colonial history, revolutionary roots, frontier expansion, and the Second Amendment.
美國普遍存在的槍支文化源自其殖民歷史、革命根源、邊疆擴張和第二修正案。

例 4

Since the Hawaiian Islands have never been connected to other land masses, the great variety of plants in Hawaii must <u>be a result of</u> the long-distance dispersal of seeds, a process that requires both a method of transport and equivalence between the ecology of the source area and that of the recipient area.

由於夏威夷群島從未與其他陸地相連，夏威夷島上種類繁多的植物必定是種子遠距離傳播的結果，傳播過程不僅需要一種傳播方式，也需要來源地和接收地的生態等位。

▶ be a result of 意思是「……的結果」。

(c) $\begin{Bmatrix} \text{ascribe} \\ \text{attribute} \\ \text{owe} \\ \text{impute} \end{Bmatrix}$ 果 (effect) to 因 (cause)

上述句型皆表示「把……歸因於」，現以「attribute 果 to 因」為例，說明如下：

❶ He attributed his success to good luck.
　▶ 句中 attributed 的受詞是「結果」，而介系詞 to 的受詞是「起因」。

His success was attributed to good luck.
他把成功歸因於好運。
　▶ 句子為被動語態，主詞是「結果」，介系詞 to 的受詞是「起因」。

❷ America's high consumption of fast food has been _____ to the fact that people are often too busy to eat a properly balanced diet.
　Ⓐ retributed　Ⓑ contributed　Ⓒ attributed　Ⓓ distributed

美國對速食的消費量很高，<u>歸因於</u>庶民經常忙到沒有時間好好吃一頓均衡的飲食。　　　　　　　　　　　　　　　　　答案：C

「impute 果 to 因」大多用在「負面」的情境（偶爾用在「正面」的情境），意思是「將（罪等）歸咎於……」。

❸ She <u>imputed</u> the project's delay <u>to</u> unexpected technical challenges.
她將專案延誤歸咎於意外的技術挑戰。

❶ due to 兩字在一起，是形容詞片語，非副詞片語，不可修飾動詞，意思是「由於……之故」。

due 的詞類是形容詞，而形容詞是用來修飾名詞，所以 due 的位置要放在名詞之前，如 the due date（【票據等的】到期日），要不然要放在 be 動詞之後當主詞補語，如「My rent is due tomorrow.（我的房租明天到期）」。

✗ <u>Due to</u> his careless driving, the accident happened.

用形容詞片語 due to... 修飾動詞 happened 的原因，是誤把形容詞片語當成副詞片語用。若有考 GMAT 的同學，在考題中若遇有 due to 的選項，一律不可選。但現在英美人士有把它當作介系詞片語用，為避免引起爭論，最好避免這種用法，建議改用介系詞片語 Owing to、Because of 或 On account of，可以當副詞來修飾動詞 happened。

題型解說　81

❶ $\left\{\begin{array}{l}\underline{\text{Owing to}}\\ \underline{\text{Because of}}\\ \underline{\text{On account of}}\end{array}\right\}$ his careless driving, the accident happened.

❷ The accident <u>was due to</u> his careless driving.

❸ The accident <u>was caused by</u> his careless driving.

　　由於他的駕駛疏忽，而引發了車禍。

　　在嚴謹的國際測驗中，due to 不當副詞片語用，但在國內英語測驗中，如：教師甄試、國家考試、研究所考試、後中西醫考試，卻屢見不鮮。下面這題教甄題的 due to 就是將形容詞片語當成副詞片語用，修飾被動動詞 hospitalized。

例

Suharto, the controversial former Indonesian president, was ____ due to failure of several internal organs this January, and he later passed away.

Ⓐ undermined　　Ⓑ stimulated

Ⓒ massacred　　Ⓓ hospitalized

備受爭議的印尼前總統蘇哈托今年一月因多重內部器官衰竭住院後與世長辭。

答案：D

J 因果關係的結構，也可以用下列動詞或動詞片語來表示：

(a) $\left\{\begin{array}{l}\text{owing to}\\ \text{because of}\\ \text{on account of}\\ \text{thanks to}\\ \text{as a result of}\end{array}\right\} + \left\{\begin{array}{l}\text{N}\\ \text{NP}\end{array}\right\}, \text{S + V}$

　　　　　　因　　　　　　　　　　果

82　Chapter 3 認識因果關係：BECAUSE 型

Thanks to 意思是「幸虧、多虧、全靠、由於、因為」，經常表示「正向、好的」理由，偶爾表達「負向、壞的」理由。根據線上辭典 Dictionary.com，thanks to 的定義是 (used to express gratitude or blame) because of; owing to，其用法是表達感謝、或譴責之意。《遠東新世紀英漢辭典》亦認為 thanks to 可以使用在壞事上，詳見以下例句。

❶ <u>Thanks to</u> your help, I succeeded.
　幸虧 / 多虧 / 全靠你的幫忙，我成功了。

❷ <u>Thanks to</u> his decision, things have come out right.
　幸虧他的果斷，形勢得以好轉。

　▶ 遠東新世紀英漢辭典

❸ The case went poorly <u>thanks to</u> the lawyer's incompetence.
　案件因律師的無能而進行得不順利。

　▶ Dictionary.com

❹ <u>Thanks to</u> bad weather, we had to put off the trip.
　由於天氣不好，我們不得不把旅行延期。

　▶ 遠東新世紀英漢辭典

相較於 thanks to，更常用 owing to, because of, on account of 等表達「負向、壞的」理由。

❶ $\begin{Bmatrix} \text{Owing to} \\ \text{Because of} \\ \text{On account of} \end{Bmatrix}$ his careless driving, the accident happened.
　由於他駕駛疏忽，而引發了車禍。

❷ As a result of the price _____ in the real estate market, an increasing number of families choose to rent houses instead of purchasing them.
   Ⓐ appreciation   Ⓑ elimination
   Ⓒ indignation   Ⓓ obstruction
   由於房地產市場價格上漲，越來越多的家庭選擇租房而不是購房。
   答案：A

(b) $\begin{Bmatrix} \text{in view of} \\ \text{in light of} \\ \text{in/by virtue of} \end{Bmatrix} + \begin{Bmatrix} \text{N} \\ \text{NP} \end{Bmatrix}, \underline{\text{S + V}}$

　　　　　　因　　　　　　　　　　　果

上述介系詞片語的意思是「鑒於、由於」。

❶ _____ the recent bombings in the England and Egypt, travelers were issued warnings to stay away from the troubled regions.
   Ⓐ In aid of   Ⓑ In case of   Ⓒ In favor of   Ⓓ In light of
   鑒於最近英國和埃及的爆炸事件，政府已發出警告提醒旅客們遠離這些動盪的地區。
   答案：D

❷ _____ drought conditions, the government decided to carry out a 36-hour water rationing scheme in both Taipei and Taoyuan.
   Ⓐ With a view to   Ⓑ In view of
   Ⓒ In case of   Ⓓ Provided that
   鑑於乾旱情況，政府決定在台北和桃園實施36小時限水計畫。
   答案：B

Ⓚ 其他表達因果關係的用法

❶ Short-term stress <u>triggers</u> the production of protective chemicals in our body and strengthens the body's defenses.
短期壓力會引發我們體內保護性化學物質的產生，增強身體的防禦能力。

▶ trigger 意思是「成為……的起因、引發……、觸發」

❷ It is the sense of inequality in the distribution of wealth that <u>breeds</u> discontent.
正是財富分配不均的感覺滋生了不滿的情緒。

▶ breed 意思是「招致、導致、引起（不良之事物）」

上下文中的線索

英語學習者是否能依據上下文推測出生詞的含義，取決於是否能找出文章中的詞彙或句構所提供的常見線索來幫助理解，而非只靠生詞或單字本身的意思，應以整句或整段的理解為主。

「因果關係」的線索（cause and effect clue）

句子或者段落中有些詞義與生詞的詞義具有因果關係，我們可以通過這種關係來推測生詞的可能意義，通常出現在表「因果」的連接詞之後，像是 since, because, so/such...that... 或者在片語之後，像是 because of, thanks to, due to, owing to, arise from, result from, result in, contribute to 等。例句已在上一節討論過。

「推斷」的線索（inference clue）

先確定生詞的詞性是名詞還是動詞等，再依據整句或整段中的其他詞如 cause (n., v.), causal (adj.); reverse (adj., v.) , reversal (n.) 等來協助了解或推斷生詞的詞義。

❶ "Never trouble trouble till trouble troubles you," is one of the best known English <u>proverbs</u>.
「麻煩沒上門，千萬莫自找」是一句有名的英諺。

▶ 四個trouble，第一個與第四是動詞，第二與第三是名詞

❷ Generally speaking, typhoons may bring heavy rain and often <u>cause</u> a lot of <u>damage</u>.
一般而言，颱風可能會帶來豪雨，常造成嚴重的損害。

❸ <u>Poverty</u> wants <u>some</u> things, <u>luxury</u> (wants) <u>many</u> things, and <u>avarice</u> (wants) <u>all</u> things.
貧窮需要一些東西，奢侈需要多東西，貪婪需要一切東西。

考古題測驗與解析

Choose the answer that best completes each sentence below.

1. The island has been hit hard by the dry seasons **as** the _____ months has been zero.

  Ⓐ precipitation　　Ⓑ conservation　　Ⓒ starvation　　Ⓓ connotation

中譯	由於全無降雨月份，這座島嶼深受乾季的嚴重影響。 Ⓐ 降水量（包括雨、雪等） Ⓑ （對自然環境的）保護；保存 Ⓒ 飢餓；餓死　　Ⓓ 隱含意義
取樣	瀏覽全文，藉標示詞as（因為）猜測前後句應呈現因果關係，取樣前半句的被動動詞片語has been hit hard by the dry seasons（深受乾季的嚴重影響）。
預測	空格內應填入和負面線索has been hit hard by the dry seasons語意緊密相關的字詞，依常理推斷，這座島嶼深受乾季的嚴重影響，必定是好幾好幾個月沒下雨了，預測選項 Ⓐ precipitation（降雨量）為可能答案。
檢驗	將 Ⓐ 選項填入空格中檢驗句意。
確認	瀏覽上下句，整體句意連貫，確認答案為 Ⓐ，正確答案就在題目上。

2. Smoking, rather than genetics, **was the cause of** his early _____.

  Ⓐ hermit　　Ⓑ demise　　Ⓒ eviction　　Ⓓ felicity

中譯	吸菸，而不是遺傳是他早逝的原因。 Ⓐ 隱士　　　　Ⓑ 終止；死亡；逝世 Ⓒ 逐出；沒收　Ⓓ 幸福；十分快樂

取樣	瀏覽全文，藉標示詞was the cause of（是……的起因）猜測前後句應呈現因果關係，取樣前半句的動名詞Smoking（吸菸）。
預測	空格內應填入和Smoking語意緊密相關的字詞，按生活經驗推斷，吸菸對身體健康有害，可能造成早逝，預測選項 ❸ demise（死亡；逝世）為可能答案。
檢驗	將 ❸ 選項填入空格中檢驗句意。
確認	瀏覽上下句，整體句意連貫，確認答案為 ❸，正確答案就在題目上。

3. Lack of rain for a period of seven months **was responsible for** the _____ of water in the reservoir.

   ❹ implicitness   ❷ abundance   ❸ attribute   ❹ depletion

中譯	連續七個月缺乏降雨導致水庫乾涸。 ❹ 含蓄 ❷ 大量；豐盛 ❸ 屬性、特性 ❹ 枯竭；耗盡
取樣	瀏覽全文，藉標示詞was responsible for（是造成……的原因）猜測前後句應呈現因果關係，取樣前半句的名詞Lack of rain（缺水）。
預測	空格內應填入和Lack of rain語意緊密相關的字詞，按生活經驗推斷，缺水會導致水庫乾枯，預測選項 ❹ depletion（枯涸）為可能答案。
檢驗	將 ❹ 選項填入空格中檢驗句意。
確認	瀏覽上下句，整體句意連貫，確認答案為 ❹，正確答案就在題目上。

4. Ten years of incompetent government has **brought about** the _____ collapse of the country's economy. It is at stake now.

Ⓐ groveling　　Ⓑ conductive　　Ⓒ radiant　　Ⓓ virtual

中譯	無能的政府執政十年已經導致國家經濟幾近崩潰。現在形勢危急。 Ⓐ 卑躬屈膝的　　Ⓑ 導電（或熱等）的 Ⓒ 容光煥發的；光芒四射的 Ⓓ 很接近的；幾乎……的；實質上的
取樣	瀏覽全文，藉標示詞brought about（引起；導致）猜測前後應呈現因果關係，取樣前半的 incompetent (government)（無能的政府）。以形容詞為解題的關鍵詞，請參閱第15頁祕訣5。另外，at stake意思是「瀕於危險」。
預測	空格內應填入和表負面「原因」incompetent (government)語意緊密相關且表負面結果的字詞，按常理來推斷，政府無能、執政長達十年，國家經濟發展會衰退，更嚴重還會導致經濟幾近崩潰，預測選項 Ⓓ virtual（幾乎……的）為可能答案。
檢驗	將 Ⓓ 選項填入空格中檢驗句意。
確認	瀏覽上下句，整體句意連貫，確認答案為 Ⓓ，正確答案就在題目上。

5. Mrs. Thomason had a _____ time last year **because of** the sudden descent of her health condition.

Ⓐ metaphorical　　Ⓑ beleaguered　　Ⓒ delectable　　Ⓓ vigorous
Ⓔ transcendent

中譯	湯瑪森太太健康狀況突然惡化，去年日子過得很艱困。 Ⓐ 隱喻的　　Ⓑ 處於困境的；受到圍困（或圍攻）的 Ⓒ 美味可口的　　Ⓓ 充滿活力的；精力充沛的 Ⓔ 卓越的；傑出的

取樣	瀏覽全文，藉標示詞because of（因為）猜測前後應呈現因果關係，取樣表「原因」的副詞片語because of 後的受詞sudden descent of her health condition（健康狀況突然惡化）。
預測	空格內應填入和負面線索sudden descent of her health condition 語意緊密相關的字詞，從生活經驗來推斷，湯瑪森太太健康狀況突然惡化，去年的日子一定過得很艱困，預測選項 **B** beleaguered（處於困境的）為可能答案。
檢驗	將 **B** 選項填入空格中檢驗句意。
確認	瀏覽上下句，整體句意連貫，確認答案為 **B**，正確答案就在題目上。

6. **Since** there are so many drug abuse cases, they are carrying out research on the causes of _____ behavior among young people.

  A defamatory   **B** inarticulate   **C** delinquent   **D** preeminent

中譯	由於毒品濫用案件層出不窮，他們正在對青少年的違法行為的原因進行研究。 **A** 誣衊的；誹謗的　　**B** 發音不清楚的、說不出的 **C** 有罪的；違法的　　**D** 卓越的；顯著的
取樣	瀏覽全文，藉標示詞since（既然）猜測前後句應呈現因果關係，取樣名詞片語 drug abuse cases（毒品濫用案件）。
預測	空格內應填入和負向線索drug abuse cases語意緊密相關的字詞，毒品濫用是違法行為，預測選項 **C** delinquent（有罪的；違法的）為可能答案。
檢驗	將 **C** 選項填入空格中檢驗句意。
確認	瀏覽上下句，整體句意連貫，確認答案為 **C**，正確答案就在題目上。

7. **Owing to** a lack of nutrition, the underprivileged children are _____ in vitamins and minerals. They appear weary and inactive, thus showing little interest in studying.

Ⓐ deficient　　Ⓑ lenient　　Ⓒ proficient　　Ⓓ omniscient

中譯	由於營養不良，這些貧童缺乏維他命和礦物質。他們顯得疲憊無力，因此對學習沒什麼興趣。 Ⓐ 缺乏的；缺少的 Ⓑ （懲罰或執法時）寬容的、仁慈的 Ⓒ 熟練的；精通的　　Ⓓ 無所不知的；全知全能的
取樣	瀏覽全文，藉標示詞owing to（因為；由於）猜測前後應呈現因果關係，取樣表「原因」的副詞片語owing to後的受詞lack of nutrition（營養不良）。
預測	空格內應填入和負面線索lack of nutrition語意緊密相關的字詞，從生活經驗來推斷，貧童營養不良，維他命和礦物質等營養素的攝取會不足夠，預測選項 Ⓐ deficient（缺乏的；不足的）為可能答案。deficiency是lack of的近義詞。
檢驗	將 Ⓐ 選項填入空格中檢驗句意。
確認	瀏覽上下句，整體句意連貫，確認答案為 Ⓐ，正確答案就在題目上。

8. The paparazzi will certainly continue to exist, **for** the public always have a(an) _____ appetite for celebrity gossip.

Ⓐ insatiable　　Ⓑ tentative　　Ⓒ discrete　　Ⓓ captious

中譯	狗仔隊一定會持續存在，因為大眾對名人八卦的愛好，總是無法滿足的。 Ⓐ （尤指慾望或需求）無法滿足的、貪得無厭的 Ⓑ 暫定的　　Ⓒ 分離的；各別的 Ⓓ 吹毛求疵的、挑剔的

取樣	瀏覽全文，藉標示詞，for（因為）猜測前後句應呈現因果關係，取樣動詞片語certainly continue to exist（肯定會持續存在）。對等連接詞for常用以表示某人推測或某人認為某事的理由，此外口語中不用for。使用for時，其前必須有標點（,）。例如：John must be ill, for he is absent today. 約翰一定生病了因為他沒有出席。（表推測的理由）
預測	空格內應填入和certainly continue to exist語意緊密相關的字詞，依生活經驗推斷，狗仔隊之所以存在是因為人們對名人八卦的愛好，是無法滿足的，預測選項 Ⓐ insatiable（（尤指慾望或需求）無法滿足的、貪得無厭的）為可能答案。
檢驗	將 Ⓐ 選項填入空格中檢驗句意。
確認	瀏覽上下句，整體句意連貫，確認答案為 Ⓐ，正確答案就在題目上。have an appetite for something意指「愛好（某物）」。

9. **With the plague severity decreasing over time**, there is little or no _____ for people to get vaccinated now.

Ⓐ deterrent　　Ⓑ turn-off　　Ⓒ resentment　　Ⓓ incentive

中譯	由於疫情的嚴重程度隨著時間降低，大家現在（幾乎）沒有誘因去接種疫苗。 Ⓐ 妨礙物；阻礙　　Ⓑ 岔道 Ⓒ 憤恨；怨恨　　Ⓓ 誘因、動機
取樣	瀏覽全文，藉With + O. + Ving（因為……）猜測前後應呈現因果關係，取樣前半的現在分詞decreasing（降低），後半的否定詞little（幾乎沒有）、no（沒有）。請參閱第13頁祕訣1。
預測	空格內應填入和decreasing語意緊密相關的字詞，依常理推斷，疫情嚴重程度隨著時間降低，現在大家（幾乎）沒有誘因去接種疫苗，預測選項 Ⓓ incentive（誘因、動機）為可能答案。
檢驗	將 Ⓓ 選項填入空格中檢驗句意。

| 確認 | 瀏覽上下句，整體句意連貫，確認答案為 **D**，正確答案就在題目上。 |

10. Ann, a prudent and sagacious teacher, always stresses the importance of thinking twice. **Thus**, her students never take a(n) _____ attitude toward her questions.

   A affluent　　**B** judicious　　**C** effulgent　　**D** flippant

中譯	安是一位既謹慎又明智的老師，她總是強調三思而後行的重要性。因此，她的學生從不對她的問題持輕率的態度。 **A** 富裕的　　　　　**B** 明智的；明斷的 **C** 燦爛的；光輝的　**D** 輕率的；無理的
取樣	瀏覽全文，藉標示詞Thus（因此）猜測前後句應呈現因果關係，取樣前句表正面「原因」的形容詞prudent and sagacious（既謹慎又明智的），和後句的否定詞never（從不）。
預測	空格內應填入和prudent and sagacious語意緊密相關的字詞，依常理推斷，老師既謹慎又睿智，學生多半不敢輕忽老師的問題，對於老師的問題必定是持謹慎態度。題目的後句也應該是表「正面」的結果，現已有否定詞never，因此選prudent的反義詞，預測選項 **D** flippant（輕率的）。prudent ≠ flippant。
檢驗	將 **D** 選項填入空格中檢驗句意。
確認	瀏覽上下句，整體句意連貫，確認答案為 **D**，正確答案就在題目上。 a prudent and sagacious teacher...Thus, ...never...flippant 　　　adj. (正)　　　　　　　　　　　　　　負　　　負 　　　　　　　　　　　　　　　　　　　　　　　　正 **注意** 四個選項，只有一個是負面的，可謂「送分題」。

11. The increasing population of the _____ cats is **due to** the irresponsible abandon of the pet owners.

Ⓐ garrulous　　**Ⓑ** feral　　**Ⓒ** jocular　　**Ⓓ** laconic

中譯	野貓數量增加是由於寵物主人的不負責任棄養所導致的。 Ⓐ（尤指在瑣事上）饒舌的、喋喋不休的 Ⓑ 野生的；未馴的　　Ⓒ 滑稽的；愛開玩笑的 Ⓓ 簡明扼要的
取樣	瀏覽全文，藉標示詞due to（因為；由於）猜測前後應呈現因果關係，取樣後半的名詞片語irresponsible abandon of the pet owners（寵物主人的不負責任棄養）。
預測	空格內應填入和負面原因線索irresponsible abandon of the pet owners語意緊密相關表結果的字詞，依常理推斷，寵物主人的不負責任棄養，會造成野貓數量的增加，預測選項 Ⓑ feral（野生的）為可能答案。
檢驗	將 Ⓑ 選項填入空格中檢驗句意。
確認	瀏覽上下句，整體句意連貫，確認答案為 Ⓑ，正確答案就在題目上。

12. Many people realized that life under the new government had become more difficult than ever before, **so that** they felt _____ for the old days.

Ⓐ nostalgic　　**Ⓑ** squeamish　　**Ⓒ** cassettes　　**Ⓓ** lorgnettes

中譯	很多人意識到在新政府統治下的生活比以往任何時候都更艱困，因此他們對過去的日子產生了懷舊之情。 Ⓐ 懷舊的；留戀過去的 Ⓑ 神經質的；（即使小事也）易受驚的 Ⓒ（錄音帶、錄影帶等的）卡式匣、盒子 Ⓓ 長柄眼鏡；（觀劇用的有柄）小型雙眼望遠鏡

取樣	瀏覽全文，藉標示詞so that（所以）猜測前後句應呈現因果關係，取樣表「原因」的前半句的動詞片語had become more difficult than ever（變得比以前更艱難）。
預測	空格內應填入和had become more difficult than ever語意緊密相關的字詞，依常理推斷，在新政府的統治下人民生活過得比以前還艱困，因此會對過往的日子（old days）產生懷舊之情，預測選項 Ⓐ nostalgic（懷舊的）為可能答案。
檢驗	將 Ⓐ 選項填入空格中檢驗句意。
確認	瀏覽上下句，整體句意連貫，確認答案為Ⓐ，因ever和the old days都提供這方面的線索，正確答案就在題目上。

13. Certain people ＿＿＿＿＿ **such** a powerful presence **that** they can absolutely captivate you within the very first moment of meeting them.

Ⓐ comport　　Ⓑ ensconce　　Ⓒ pillage　　Ⓓ exude

中譯	有些人散發出如此強大的氣場，以致於能讓你在初次見到他們的那一刻就完全著迷。 Ⓐ 行為表現；舉止　　Ⓑ 安置；使安頓 Ⓒ 搶劫；掠奪　　　　Ⓓ 滲出（液體）；散發出（氣味）
取樣	瀏覽全文，藉標示詞such...that（如此……以致於）猜測前後句應呈現因果關係，取樣名詞片語powerful presence（強大的氣場）、動詞片語absolutely captivate you（讓你完全著迷）。
預測	根據句構和選項得知空格內要填入動詞，such a powerful presence是當該動詞的受詞，前半句的such a powerful presence表「正面」的原因，後半句的absolutely captivate you表「正面」的結果，因此空格內需填入符合語義，不影響因果關係的動詞，預測選項 Ⓓ exude（散發出）為可能答案。
檢驗	將 Ⓓ 選項填入空格中檢驗句意。
確認	瀏覽上下句，整體句意連貫，確認答案為 Ⓓ，正確答案就在題目上。

考古題測驗與解析 95

14. Employees had become **so** inured to the caprices of top management's personnel policies **that** they greeted the announcement of a company-wide dress code with _____.

Ⓐ hostility　　**Ⓑ** confusion　　**Ⓒ** resentment　　**Ⓓ** impassivity

中譯	員工已經非常習慣最高管理階層人事政策反覆無常，以致於他們對公司全面實施的服裝規定公告無動於衷。 Ⓐ 敵意　　　　Ⓑ 混亂；混淆 Ⓒ 憤恨；怨恨　　Ⓓ 無動於衷；冷漠
取樣	瀏覽全文，藉標示詞so...that（如此……以致於）猜測前後應呈現因果關係，取樣表「原因」的形容詞片語inured to the caprices of top management's personnel policies（習慣最高管理階層人事政策反覆無常）。 **注意** inure (vt)〔常用被動語態〕使習慣於。
預測	空格內應填入和負面線索inured to the caprices of top management's personnel policies語意緊密相關表負面結果的字詞，從常理來推斷，員工已經習慣最高管理階層人事政策的反覆無常，對於公司的服裝新規定必定無感，習以為常，甚至表現出冷漠的態度，預測選項 Ⓓ impassivity（無動於衷）為可能答案。
檢驗	將 Ⓓ 選項填入空格中檢驗句意。
確認	瀏覽上下句，整體句意連貫，確認答案為 Ⓓ，正確答案就在題目上。

15. Since the 18th century, California's kelp forest has been steadily mowed down by purple urchins, **thanks to** the _____ of their natural predator–the sea otter.

Ⓐ progress　　**Ⓑ** salvage　　**Ⓒ** relief　　**Ⓓ** massacre

中譯	由於大規模屠殺了牠們的天敵——海獺，自從十八世紀以來，加利福尼亞的海帶森林不斷地遭受紫海膽的大肆破壞。 Ⓐ 進步；進展　Ⓑ（對財物等的）搶救 Ⓒ（難民、貧民等的）救濟、救濟物品； 　（痛苦、憂慮等的）解除、減輕 Ⓓ 大屠殺；（牲畜的）成批屠宰
取樣	瀏覽全文，藉標示詞thanks to（因為；由於）猜測前後應呈現因果關係。解題時，看到adj.+ly + Vp.p.這樣的結構往往是重點，要優先取樣，因此取樣前半的動詞片語steadily mowed down（不斷地遭受……大肆破壞）。參閱第16頁祕訣6。
預測	空格內應填入表「負面」結果與steadily mowed down有關「負面」原因的字詞，依常理推斷，海帶森林不斷地遭受紫海膽的大肆破壞是因為紫海膽的天敵——海獺，被大規模屠殺，預測選項 Ⓓ massacre（大屠殺）為可能答案。
檢驗	將 Ⓓ 選項填入空格中檢驗句意。
確認	瀏覽上下句，整體句意連貫，確認答案為 Ⓓ，正確答案就在題目上。

16. The Chinese had been repeatedly defeated in war in the Qing Dynasty. The _____ paid to the winners **led to** the bankruptcy of the empire.

Ⓐ integrity　Ⓑ epiphany　Ⓒ indemnity　Ⓓ equanimity

中譯	清朝時期，中國在戰爭中連連戰敗，支付賠款給戰勝國，導致了帝國的破產。 Ⓐ 誠實正直；完整 Ⓑ（神的）顯現；（對事物真意的）領悟 Ⓒ（對於損害或損失的）賠償；賠款 Ⓓ（尤指處於困境時的）鎮靜、沉著、冷靜

取樣	瀏覽全文，藉標示詞led to（引起；導致），猜測前後應呈現因果關係，取樣後半的表「結果」的名詞片語bankruptcy of the empire（帝國的破產）。
預測	空格內應填入和表「負面」結果bankruptcy of the empire語意緊密相關的字詞，依常理推斷，戰爭失敗需賠款給戰勝國可能導致帝國的破產，預測選項 **C** indemnity（賠款）為可能答案。
檢驗	將 **C** 選項填入空格中檢驗句意。
確認	瀏覽上下句，整體句意連貫，確認答案為 **C**，正確答案就在題目上。

17. We are responsible for the disruption of the climate and for the dangerous world that we are going to _____ to our children. **Therefore**, we should take action to protect the earth.

   A exonerate　　**B** bequeath　　**C** concoct　　**D** confiscate

中譯	我們要為氣候的破壞、留給後代危險的世界負責。因此，我們應該採取行動來保護地球。 **A** 宣佈（某人）無罪；免除（責任、義務）等 **B** （在遺囑中）把……遺贈給；遺留給；傳給後代 **C** 配製（尤指食物或飲料）；編造（故事、藉口等） **D** （尤指作為懲罰）沒收、把……充公
取樣	瀏覽全文，藉標示詞Therefore（因此）猜測前後句應呈現因果關係，取樣第二句表「結果」的動詞片語take action to protect the earth（採取行動來保護地球）。
預測	空格內應填入和take action to protect the earth有關表「原因」相關的字詞，作者認為我們要為氣候的破壞及我們將留給後代的危險世界負責，因此應該採取行動來保護地球，預測選項 **B** bequeath（遺留給；傳給後代）為可能答案。
檢驗	將 **B** 選項填入空格中檢驗句意。

| 確認 | 瀏覽上下句，整體句意連貫，確認答案為 Ⓑ，正確答案就在題目上。 |

18. Wrinkles **result from** the loss of _____ that goes naturally with aging, causing the skin to sag and crumple.

    Ⓐ electricity　　Ⓑ ecstasy　　Ⓒ empathy　　Ⓓ elasticity

中譯	皺紋是由於隨著年齡增長，皮膚自然失去<u>彈性</u>所致，導致皮膚下垂和皺縮。 Ⓐ 電；電能　　　　　　Ⓑ 狂喜；陶醉 Ⓒ 同感；（心理）同理心　Ⓓ 彈性；彈力
取樣	瀏覽全文，藉標示詞 result form（（因……）發生；（隨……）產生）猜測前後應呈現因果關係，取樣表「結果」的名詞 Wrinkles（皺紋）。
預測	空格內應填入和 Wrinkles 語意相關表「原因」的字詞，依生活經驗推斷，皺紋的產生是和年齡增長，皮膚失去彈性所致，預測選項 Ⓓ elasticity（彈性；彈力）為可能答案。
檢驗	將 Ⓓ 選項填入空格中檢驗句意。
確認	瀏覽上下句，整體句意連貫，確認答案為 Ⓓ，正確答案就在題目上。

19. The rise in juvenile crime these years in Taiwan has **been attributed to** the _____ of the family system and the competitive education system.

    Ⓐ deterioration　　Ⓑ transgression　　Ⓒ verification　　Ⓓ prosecution

中譯	這些年來台灣青少年犯罪增加，<u>歸因於</u>家庭制度的變質和競爭激烈的教育體制。 Ⓐ 惡化、變質　　Ⓑ 違犯、犯罪 Ⓒ 確認、證實　　Ⓓ 起訴；檢舉

考古題測驗與解析　99

取樣	瀏覽全文，藉標示詞been attributed to（歸因於）猜測前後應呈現因果關係，取樣表「結果」的名詞片語The rise in juvenile crime（青少年犯罪的增加）。
預測	空格內應填入和The rise in juvenile crime語意相關表「原因」的字詞，依生活經驗推斷，台灣青少年犯罪增加，多半是家庭和學校功能變質所致，預測選項 Ⓐ deterioration（惡化、變質）為可能答案。
檢驗	將 Ⓐ 選項填入空格中檢驗句意。
確認	瀏覽上下句，整體句意連貫，確認答案為 Ⓐ，正確答案就在題目上。

20. Some web sites are full of _____, **so** we've put a filter on our computer to keep our children from these immoral sites.

　　Ⓐ depravity　　Ⓑ scrambling　　Ⓒ aviation　　Ⓓ resolution

中譯	有些網站充滿著<u>傷風敗俗的內容</u>，因此我們在電腦上安裝過濾軟體，以防孩子進入這些不道德的網站。 Ⓐ 道德敗壞、墮落　　Ⓑ 爬行 Ⓒ 航空；飛行　　Ⓓ 決意、決心（之事）
取樣	瀏覽全文，藉標示詞so（所以）猜測前後句應呈現因果關係，取樣後句表「結果」的動詞片語put a filter（安裝過濾軟體）與表「目的」的不定詞片語to keep our children from these immoral sites（以防孩子進入這些不道德的網站）。
預測	從後句的put a filter和immoral sites得知，網頁上必定是有不適合孩子接觸的內容才會安裝過濾軟體，因此空格應填入一個表達「負面」含義的名詞，預測選項 Ⓐ depravity（道德敗壞、墮落）是唯一表「負面」含義的答案。
檢驗	將 Ⓐ 選項填入空格中檢驗句意。
確認	瀏覽上下句，整體句意連貫，確認答案為 Ⓐ，正確答案就在題目上。

21. Dramatic literature often _____ the history of a culture **in that** it takes as its subject matter the important events that have shaped and guided the culture.

Ⓐ anticipates **Ⓑ** recapitulates **Ⓒ** repudiates **Ⓓ** polarizes
Ⓔ confounds

中譯	戲劇文學通常會扼要重述文化的歷史，因為戲劇文學會把塑造和引導該文化的重要事件視為主題。 Ⓐ 預料；預期　　Ⓑ 扼要的重述；概括 Ⓒ 拒絕（要求等）；不承認；駁斥 Ⓓ （使）兩極化，截然對立　　Ⓔ 使困惑；使混淆
取樣	瀏覽全文，藉標示詞in that（因為）猜測前後句應呈現因果關係，取樣後句的名詞片語subject matter（主題）。為什麼取樣subject matter呢？因為受詞補語（objective complement）可以補足受詞意義上的不足，這就形成整句語意的焦點，也就成了該句的關鍵詞。 **注意** 副詞子句in that it takes as <u>its subject matter the important events that have shaped and guided the culture</u>.是從 in that it takes <u>the important events that have shaped and guided the culture as its subject matter</u>. 演變而來的，句中的take A(O) as B(OC)的用法，意思是「將A視為B」，例如：She took his advice <u>as</u> a personal attack on her abilities.（她把他的建議當作對她能力的人身攻擊。）但因為take後所接的受詞太長，讀者無法輕易理解該句，因此將較長的受詞放到句尾，這個概念稱為「尾重原則」（end-weight principle）。 為讓讀者更清楚了解何謂「尾重原則」，請見底下的例句和說明：<u>A big blue pitcher full of warm milk</u> was on the table.（桌上有一大罐盛滿溫牛奶的藍色水壺。）這個句子雖然沒有文法錯誤，但因為主詞A big blue pitcher full of warm milk 過長，給人頭重腳輕之感，因此將主詞移到句尾，將地方副詞on the table移到句首，形成倒裝句On the table was <u>a big blue pitcher full of warm milk</u>.。相信讀者從這個例句中，能夠清楚看到「尾重原則」指的是較長的結構放在較短的結構之後。在這個例句中，長的名詞片語（a big blue pitcher full of warm milk）

	出現在句子的末尾，讀者先讀短的訊息，再讀長的訊息，會更容易容易理解句意。
預測	從後句得知戲劇文學以塑造和引導該文化的重要事件為主題（as its subject matter），主題就是本句語意焦點，請參閱第14頁祕訣4，而本句主題指的就是the important events that have shaped and guided the culture，因此戲劇文學不可避免地會扼要重述這一個文化的歷史，預測選項 Ⓑ recapitulates（重述；概括）為可能答案。
檢驗	將 Ⓑ 選項填入空格中檢驗句意。
確認	瀏覽上下句，整體句意連貫，確認答案為 Ⓑ，正確答案就在題目上。

22. This region is **so** damp **that** moisture seems to _____ everything. Towels wouldn't dry and windows are always foggy.

    Ⓐ perpetrate　　Ⓑ permeate　　Ⓒ proliferate　　Ⓓ perspire

中譯	這個地區濕氣太重，濕氣彷彿滲透了一切。毛巾乾不了，窗戶總是霧濛濛的。 Ⓐ 犯（罪）；做（錯事）　　Ⓑ 滲透；瀰漫 Ⓒ 迅速繁殖（或增殖）；猛增　　Ⓓ 出汗；排汗
取樣	瀏覽全文，藉標示詞so...that（如此……以致於）猜測前後應呈現因果關係，取樣表「原因」的形容詞damp（潮濕的；溼氣重的）。參閱第13頁祕訣2。
預測	空格內應填入和負面原因damp語意緊密相關的字詞，從生活經驗來判斷，溼氣重的地區，濕氣會滲透一切，溼答答的，預測選項 Ⓑ permeate（滲透；瀰漫）為可能答案。
檢驗	將 Ⓑ 選項填入空格中檢驗句意。
確認	瀏覽上下句，整體句意連貫，確認答案為 Ⓑ，正確答案就在題目上。

23. Art as therapy is considered product-oriented **because** it's satisfying to create a piece of art that is _____ pleasing.

Ⓐ aerobically　　Ⓑ atheistically　　Ⓒ aseptically　　Ⓓ athletically
Ⓔ aesthetically

中譯	藝術治療被視為是以產品為導向的，因為創造出一件美觀的藝術品能讓病患得到滿足感。 Ⓐ 有氧地　　Ⓑ 無神論地　　Ⓒ 無（病）菌地 Ⓓ 強壯地　　Ⓔ 審美地
取樣	瀏覽全文，藉標示詞because（因為）猜測前後句應呈現因果關係，取樣表「結果」的主要子句中的名詞Art as therapy（藝術治療）和表「原因」副詞子句中的形容詞子句pleasing。
預測	空格內應填入和Art as therapy、pleasing語意緊密相關的副詞，按常理推斷，當病患看到一件創造出來的藝術品，覺得很滿意（pleasing）、很舒適，那件藝術品一定有「藝術美」，預測選項 Ⓔ aesthetically（審美地）為可能答案。
檢驗	將 Ⓔ 選項填入空格中檢驗句意。
確認	瀏覽上下句，整體句意連貫，檢視四個選項，只有副詞Ⓔ與「美」有關，修飾pleasing，確認答案為Ⓔ，正確答案就在題目上。

24. A batch of sodium chloride manufactured by Y F Chemical Corp. was _____ with bacteria, **resulting in** fevers for eight patients after they were injected with the solution.

Ⓐ purified　　Ⓑ disinfected　　Ⓒ obstructed　　Ⓓ confined
Ⓔ tainted

中譯	一批由 YF化學公司製造的氯化鈉受到細菌汙染，導致八名患者在注射該溶液後發燒。 Ⓐ 使（某物）潔淨；淨化　　Ⓑ 給……消毒 Ⓒ 阻擋；阻塞　　Ⓓ 限制；限定　　Ⓔ 使腐壞；汙染
取樣	瀏覽全文，藉標示詞resulting in（造成；導致）猜測前後應呈現因果關係，取樣表「結果」的片語中的名詞fevers（發燒）。
預測	空格內應填入表「負面」結果fevers有關表「原因」的字詞，依醫學常識來推斷，如果施打受到細菌汙染的氯化鈉溶劑會引起發燒，預測選項 Ⓔ tainted（汙染）為可能答案。
檢驗	將 Ⓔ 選項填入空格中檢驗句意。
確認	瀏覽上下句，整體句意連貫，確認答案為 Ⓔ，正確答案就在題目上。

25. According to Leo Tolstoy, "art" in our modern society has become **so** _____ **that** not only has bad art come to be considered good, but even the very perception of what art really is has lost.

Ⓐ germane Ⓑ perverted Ⓒ benevolent Ⓓ rebarbative

中譯	根據列夫·托爾斯泰的觀點，在我們現代社會裡，「藝術」已經變得如此<u>扭曲</u>，以致於不僅有人認為糟糕的藝術是好的，甚至也喪失了那種對真正藝術的認知。 Ⓐ（議論等）切題的；關係貼切的；（比喻等）貼切的 Ⓑ 被扭曲的；被曲解的　　Ⓒ 慈善的；行善的 Ⓓ 猙獰的；令人厭惡的
取樣	瀏覽全文，藉標示詞so...that（如此……以致於）猜測前後應呈現因果關係，取樣表「結果」的名詞片語bad art（糟糕的藝術）語意焦點在bad、被動動詞be considered good（認為是好的）語意焦點在good、名詞片語the very perception（那種認知）、動詞has lost（喪失）。
預測	空格內應填入和負面線索bad art、be considered good和very perception、has lost語意緊密相關的字詞，按常理來說，糟糕的藝術被認為是好的，對真正藝術的認知也喪失，表示現代社會對於藝術的看法（bad art）已經扭曲成（good art），預測選項 Ⓑ perverted（被扭曲的）為可能答案。參閱第14頁祕訣4、第19頁祕訣10。
檢驗	將 Ⓑ 選項填入空格中檢驗句意。
確認	瀏覽上下句，整體句意連貫，確認答案為 Ⓑ，正確答案就在題目上。

實戰練習

1. Thousands of people flooded into the city to join the demonstration; **as a result**, the city's transportation system was almost _____.

   Ⓐ testified   Ⓑ paralyzed   Ⓒ stabilized   Ⓓ dissatisfied

2. The presidential candidate apologized _____ for her inappropriate remarks on racial issues, **so** her support rate went up five points.

   Ⓐ capriciously   Ⓑ obstinately   Ⓒ truculently   Ⓓ profusely

3. As the new NHS pension scheme takes effect, doctors in England are now being asked to work even longer and to contribute much more of their salary. **Hence**, they are taking steps against the UK government because they think this _____ government is making unnecessary changes to the NHS pension scheme and unwilling to negotiate.

   Ⓐ intransigent   Ⓑ jovial   Ⓒ prognostic   Ⓓ surreptitious

4. It was her view that the country's problems had been _____ by foreign technocrats, **so that** to invite them to come back would be counterproductive.

   Ⓐ attacked   Ⓑ exacerbated   Ⓒ ascertained   Ⓓ foreseen

5. He was in **such** a _____ **that** he didn't know whether to advance or retreat.

   Ⓐ predilection   Ⓑ attainment   Ⓒ predicament   Ⓓ complacency

6. **As** there is no free lunch in diplomacy, suspicions remain that financial aid promised by China has been a _____ for the aid-receiving countries' support on China's territorial claim on disputed waters.

   Ⓐ coup d'état   Ⓑ carte blanche   Ⓒ quid pro quo   Ⓓ cul-de-sac

7. Some academic conference events were attended **because of** their potential for _____ rather than as an imperative for research.

   Ⓐ leisure　Ⓑ boycott　Ⓒ treasury　Ⓓ measure

8. The British pound has _____ against the US dollar considerably in recent weeks **due to** the result of the Brexit referendum. That is, the pound has become cheaper.

   Ⓐ deflated　Ⓑ decreased　Ⓒ despaired　Ⓓ depreciated

9. The artist's tireless dedication to his craft **resulted in** a(n) _____ of work that was both beautiful and thought-provoking.

   Ⓐ blunder　Ⓑ debris　Ⓒ eclipse　Ⓓ opus

10. He was grilled by detectives for two hours **because** he _____ bought a car stolen from an old lady a few days ago.

   Ⓐ grotesquely　Ⓑ unwittingly　Ⓒ premedically　Ⓓ turbulently

11. Prices and inventory levels _____ considerably from week to week, in part predictably (e.g., **due to** seasonal shifts in demand) and in part unpredictably.

   Ⓐ merge　Ⓑ vibrate　Ⓒ fluctuate　Ⓓ move

12. When Patricia walked out to the beach for a stroll, she could hardly open her eyes **because of** the _____ sunlight.

   Ⓐ ejecting　Ⓑ glaring　Ⓒ jeering　Ⓓ ousting

解答

1. Ⓑ　2. Ⓓ　3. Ⓐ　4. Ⓑ　5. Ⓒ　6. Ⓒ　7. Ⓐ　8. Ⓓ　9. Ⓓ　10. Ⓑ
11. Ⓒ　12. Ⓑ

Chapter 4

認識並列結構：

AND 型

題型解說

And 型【並列結構（equality of ideas）】

如何翻譯 And

不要一見到 "and" 就譯為中文「和」、「跟」、「與」等字。

❶ And 連接名詞：一般只有 and 在連接兩個名詞時才會用「和」、「跟」、「與」等字，甚至也可省略不譯，如：人有悲歡離合，月有陰晴圓缺，此事古難全。

例1 Time and tide wait for no men.
時間與潮汐不等人。 ⎫
光陰潮汐不待人。 ⎭ →歲月不待人。

▶ time與tide：名詞平行排比或平行對稱

例2 Books and friends should be few but good.
書本與朋友宜少宜精。 ⎫
書籍朋友要少但要好。 ⎭ →書與友不在多而在精；廣交不如擇友。

▶ books與friends：名詞平行排比或平行對稱

例3 Age and experience teach wisdom.
年齡與歷練增人智。

例4 Sticks and stones may break my bones, but words may never hurt me.
木頭石頭可以打斷我骨頭，謾罵絕對傷不了我。→笑罵由他笑罵。

例5 There are people and people.
人有千百種。→好的壞的都有。

例6 Bread and butter is fattening.
✗ 奶油和麵包會使人發胖。
○ 奶油麵包會使人發胖。

❷ And 連接動詞或動名詞：不可以譯成「和」，有時也可以省略不譯。例如：

例1 Forget and forgive.
寬恕而後忘記。→不念舊惡，既往不咎。

例2 Live and learn.
活著就要學習。→活到老，學到老。

例3 We drank and sang merrily.
👎 我們高興地喝酒和唱歌。
👍 我們高興地又喝酒又唱歌／我們高興地喝酒唱歌。

例4 Dicing, drabbing, and drinking are the three D's to destruction.
賭、嫖、酒是三個致命傷。

▶ dicing、drabbing與drinking：動名詞平行對稱

❸ And 連接形容詞、副詞、片語：And 連接形容詞，不宜譯成「和」、「跟」，可譯成「又……又」、「既……又」、「既……且」、「且」。

例1 John is intelligent and diligent.
👎 約翰聰明和勤勉。
👍 約翰既聰明又勤勉。

例2 The train ran quickly and smoothly.
火車行駛得又快又穩／火車行駛得既快且穩。

例3 Early to bed and early to rise makes a man healthy, wealthy, and wise.
早睡早起使人健康、富有、（又）聰明。

題型解說 111

❹ And 連接句子更不可譯成「和」，應視情況省略或變通。

例1 The soldiers constructed a bridge <u>and</u> (they) brought the cannons across the river.
士兵築了橋，<u>然後</u>把大砲運過河。

例2 Marriage halves our grief, doubles our joy, <u>and</u> quadruples our expenses.
結婚使憂愁減半，歡樂加倍，開銷加四倍。

例3 The father buys, the son builds, the grandson sells, <u>and</u> his son begs.
父買地，子建地，孫賣地，曾孫行乞。→富不過三代。

例4 Young men look forward, the middle-aged look around, <u>and</u> old men look back.
年輕人眺望未來，中年人瞻前顧後，老年人回首憶往。

分析並列結構（equality of ideas）

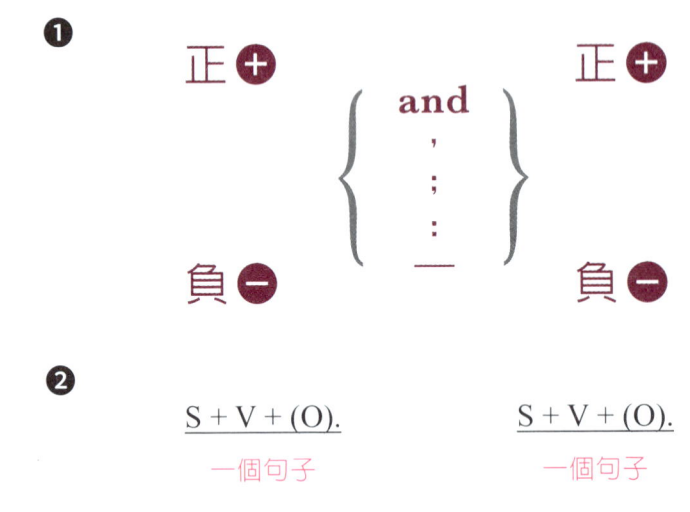

❶

正➕　　　　　　　　　　正➕

　　　　{ and , ; ─ }

負➖　　　　　　　　　　負➖

❷

　　S + V + (O).　　　　S + V + (O).
　　　一個句子　　　　　　一個句子

前後二個句子，請參考 116 頁「補充說明」的線索。

112　Chapter 4　認識並列結構：AND 型

> 說明

　　句中若用對等連接詞 and、逗號（,）、分號（;）、冒號（:）或破折號（一）連接兩部分，這兩部份意義必須一致或平行，譬如二則均為正面意義或二則均為反面意義。類似的連結關係，除 and 外，還包括 not only...but also...、as well as 等。此外分號（semicolon）可以代替對等連接詞，連接兩個關係密切（closely related）的字句。至於冒號（:）通常用於解說第一個主要子句的第二個主要子句之前。

A Learning without thought is labor lost; thought without learning is perilous.
學而不思則罔；思而不學則殆。

B The humane man, desiring to be established himself, seeks to establish others; desiring himself to succeed, he helps others to succeed.
己欲立而立人；己欲達而達人。

C We have had to abandon our holiday plans: the dates didn't work out.
我們必須放棄休假的計畫：日期沒有弄好。

D Her intention is obvious: she wants to marry him.
她的意圖很明顯：她就是要嫁給他。

E Our building has 24-hour security <u>as well as</u> a very helpful concierge.
我們的大樓擁有24小時的保全以及非常樂於助人的管理員。

F <u>Neither</u> auditory hallucination <u>nor</u> delusion is his symptom, so I think he is far from schizophrenia.
他既沒有幻覺，也沒有妄想的症狀，所以我認為他絕非罹患思覺失調症。

其他應注意之處

❶ 避免主詞曖昧不明，無法讓讀者意會主詞是誰。因此，為了維持接續的功能，前後二句的主詞最好一致。沒必要，不可隨便轉移。

a) 👎 John returned to Taiwan. <u>Numerous buildings</u> along Taipei streets were seen.
   👍 John returned to Taiwan. <u>He</u> saw numerous buildings along Taipei streets.
   約翰回到了台灣。他看到台北街頭的許多建築物。

b) 👎 John arrived in Taipei and many skyscrapers came into his sight.
   👍 John arrived in Taipei and saw many skyscrapers.
   約翰抵達台北，看到了許多摩天大樓。

❷ This / that 可代替前面已經說過的句子或子句，以避免重複。

a) <u>He always got up at nine</u>. <u>This</u> made him a very lazy man.
   (=He always got up at nine. That he always got up at nine made him a very lazy man.)
   他總是九點起床，這樣使他成為一個很懶的人。

This 是代替前面的句子 "He always got up at nine." 做後面句子裡動詞 <u>made</u> 的主詞。

b) He will give his vote to me, but <u>that</u> is not enough.
   (=He will give his vote to me, but that he will give his vote to me is not enough.)
   他願意投我一票，但那是不夠的。

that 是代替前面的句子 "He will give his vote to me," 做後面句子裡動詞 <u>is</u> 的主詞。

上下文中的線索

英語學習者是否能依據上下文推測出生詞的含義，取決於是否能找出文章中的詞彙或句構所提供常見的線索來幫助理解，而非只靠生詞或單字本身的意思，應以整句或整段的理解為主。

「定義」的線索（definition clue）

作者為幫助讀者理解生詞，常常在文句中下定義，因此讀者應注意提示生詞定義的相關字詞，如接在現在式動詞 mean, be defined as, be known as, be called, be considered, refer to, is, are 等之後，或在解釋性的片語（如 that is (to say), in other words, namely 等）之後。例如：

❶ The red light means "stop".
紅燈表示「停」。

❷ Creativity by definition means going against the tradition and breaking the rules.
創造力的定義是違背傳統，打破規則。

❸ Triangle is defined as a plain figure with three sides and three angles.
三角形的定義是有三個邊和三個角的平面圖形。

❹ What do these numbers refer to?
這些數字表示什麼意思？

❺ Self-knowledge refers to the ability to know what we know and what we do not know.
自我認知指的是瞭解自己知道什麼以及不知道什麼的能力。

❻ A professor is a teacher of the highest rank in a university.
教授是大學裡最高職位的教師。

❼ Synesthesia is a condition in which people's senses intermix.
聯覺是一種人的感官感受混合在一起的狀況。

❽ There is nothing that costs less than civility. In other words, courtesy costs nothing.
沒有比禮貌更不要花錢的；換言之，禮貌不用花錢。

▶ 以禮待人，貴而不貴

❾ In the post-truth era, facts are less significant in shaping public viewpoint than appeals to emotion and personal belief. In other words, the truth is pictured elusively. It is easy to examine the data and come to any conclusion you desire.
在後真相時代，相對於訴諸情感和個人信仰，事實在形塑公眾觀點上不是那麼的重要。換句話說，真相被描繪成難以捉摸的。分析資料並得出任何你想要的結論是很容易的事。

❿ With the advancement of technology, mobile phones have become increasingly available and inexpensive. That is, the handy little gadgets have been _____.

Ⓐ indigenous　Ⓑ euphonious

Ⓒ ostentatious　Ⓓ ubiquitous

隨著科技的進步，手機已經變得越來越普及且便宜。也就是說，這些方便的小玩意已經無所不在了。　　　　　答案：D

「補充說明」的線索（explanation clue）

有時生詞的詞義可能出現在比下定義略長的補充說明句中，該句可能是另一句，如下列前三句，或句中用分號（;）如 ⓬～⓭ 句、逗號（,）如 ❹～❻ 句、冒號（:）如 ❼ 句、括弧如 ⓫ 句，或引號提示的某一部分，如 ❾～❿ 句。

❶ While rental costs go higher in California, <u>eviction</u> from rental housing is also a problem. Activists say some landlords have forced people to move from rental units so they can be offered to tech workers, who will pay a higher price.

加州租金上漲的同時，租客被趕出租屋處也是個問題。有活動人士表示，有些房東迫使房客搬離租賃單位，以便將其出租給科技從業者，因他們願意支付較高的房租。

❷ According to a Legatum Institute's survey, Norway is the most _____ nation in the world. This Scandinavian country has claimed the top spot over 142 most flourishing countries for six years in a row.

Ⓐ inflating　　Ⓑ unoriginal

Ⓒ prosperous　Ⓓ conventional

根據列格坦研究機構的調查，挪威是世界上最繁榮的國家。這個斯堪地那維亞國家在142個最繁榮的國家中連續六年蟬聯榜首。

▶答案：C

❸ The researchers had divergent opinions on the factors that contribute to aging. The findings of their studies were _____.

Ⓐ synonymous　Ⓑ formidable

Ⓒ indigenous　　Ⓓ equivocal

研究人員對於導致老化的因素意見分歧。他們研究的結果並不明確。

▶答案：D

❹ He has absolutely no scruples, <u>no morals</u>; he'll do anything to get what he wants.

他毫無顧忌，沒有道德；他會不擇手段地得到他想要的東西。

❺ Most dictionaries give the <u>etymology</u>, <u>or</u> the origin, of each word. 大部分辭典都提供「字源」，<u>也就是</u>字的肇始。

▶ 不要一見到"or"就譯成「或者」。or之前若有逗號（,）可譯成「亦即、也就是、換句話說」（that is, that means）。

上下文中的線索　117

❻ Cultural evolution, or the adaptive changes of cultures in response to changes in the environment over time, is possible only because humans have been genetically endowed with a capacity for learning and language.

只是因為人類天生具備學習和語言能力，才有可能發生文化演化，也就是文化隨著時間的推移，因應環境變化而做出的適應性變化。

❼ Many artists in the Renaissance worked, as Leonardo did, in a wide variety of media: drawing, painting, sculpture, architecture and so forth.

許多文藝復興時期的藝術家，如同李奧納多一樣，涉獵廣泛的媒材，例如：繪畫、雕塑、建築等等。

❽ I like a variety of music genres: country, classical, jazz, alternative, and folk music.

我喜歡各種音樂流派：鄉村音樂、古典音樂、爵士音樂、另類音樂和民謠音樂。

❾ In the recent meeting, Xi said that China aimed to cooperate with Russia, and Putin likewise praised the "multifaceted ties" they have forged.

在最近的會議上，習近平說中國打算與俄羅斯合作，而普丁也稱讚他們所建立的「多面向的關係」。

❿ But sometime in the 1760s, the merchant class of Paris developed a taste for healthy clear broths which were considered restorative; hence the term "restaurant."

但在18世紀60年代的某個時候，巴黎的商賈階級開始喜歡上對健康有益的清湯，大家認為這種湯能恢復精力（restorative）；因此出現了「餐廳（restaurant）」這個詞。

⓫ In "perfect weather", the humidity (moisture in the air) is about 65 percent.

「完美天氣」的濕度（空氣中的水氣）約為百分之六十五。

> **說明**
>
> humidity 是一個生詞，但它後面的括弧內對其含義進行解釋（moisture in the air）。

⑫ The child is a prodigy; he entered college at the age of ten.
這個孩子是神童；十歲就上大學了。

⑬ The most distant luminous objects seen by telescopes are probably ten thousand million light years away; the light from the nearby Virgo galaxy set out when reptiles still were prevalent in the animal world.
望遠鏡所觀測到最遙遠的發光物體可能距離我們一百億光年遠；而來自鄰近處女座銀河系的光線是在爬行動物仍然普遍存在於動物界時發射出來的。

「實例解釋」的線索（example clue）

　　生詞的含義也可從文中通俗易懂的例子，藉日常生活的經驗所提供的常識來推斷。舉例時一般會用到的詞語：such as 如❶句、for example 如❷句、for instance 如❸句、including 如❹句以及 especially 如❺句等。為了強調或解釋某一事物，作者常常會在括弧內如❻、❼句，或者破折號（—）後對生詞進行解釋，如❽句，逗號（,）或縮略字如 e.g. (=for example) 如❾和❿句，i.e. (=that is/in other words) 如⓫、⑫句等。

❶ Bill Gates now spends his time on many altruistic projects <u>such as</u> charity work.
比爾・蓋茲現在將時間花在許多利他計畫上，<u>例如</u>慈善工作。

上下文中的線索 119

❷ Many numbers are associated with superstitious beliefs. <u>For example</u>, thirteen is said to be an unlucky number in Western countries.
許多數字與迷信觀念有關。<u>例如</u>，據說十三在西方國家是不吉利的數字。

❸ The new manager is very demanding. <u>For instance</u>, the employees are given much shorter deadlines for the same tasks than before.
新上任的經理要求很高，舉例來說，相同的工作，給員工的最後期限卻比以前短很多。

❹ Most people infected with the MERS virus developed severe respiratory illness <u>including</u> symptoms such as fever, cough and shortness of breath.
大多數感染中東呼吸症候群冠狀病毒感染症（MERS）的人會出現嚴重的呼吸道疾病，包括發燒、咳嗽和呼吸急促等症狀。

❺ He likes all extracurricular activities, <u>especially</u> basketball playing.
他喜歡所有的課外活動，尤其是打籃球。

❻ The <u>colors</u> of the flag (<u>red</u>, <u>yellow</u> and <u>white</u>) decorated convention center.
那旗幟的顏色（紅、黃、白）裝飾了大會中心。

❼ In the 1980s, most archaeologists believed that a young leader named Pachacuti Inca Yupanqui (also known as <u>Pachacutec</u>) became the first Inca king in the early 1400s.
在1980年代，大多數考古學家認為一位名叫帕查庫特克‧因卡‧尤潘基（又稱帕查庫特克）的年輕領袖，在15世紀初成為了第一位印加國王。

❽ Not until she was married to him did she discover what he truly was in his sordid past—drug dealer and enforcer in a crime syndicate.

直到嫁給他，她才發現他骯髒過去的真實身份——毒品販子和犯罪集團的打手。

❾ <u>Minerals</u> are important to our bodies, e.g. <u>calcium and sodium</u>.
礦物質對我們身體很重要，例如鈣、鈉等。

> **說明**
>
> e.g. = (拉丁語) exempli gratia，表例如 (=for example)。將「e.g.」後面的詞彙作為實例用來解說「e.g.」前面的詞彙。

❿ Most cases of avian influenza infection in humans have resulted from contact with infected <u>poultry</u> (e.g., <u>domesticated chicken, ducks, and turkeys</u>) or surfaces contaminated with secretions from infected birds.
人類感染禽流感的大多數案例都是接觸受感染的禽鳥（例如家雞、鴨和火雞）或接觸受感染鳥類分泌物汙染的表面所致。

⓫ The film is meant only for <u>adults</u>, i.e. <u>people over 18</u>.
這部電影是成人電影，換言之，只限18歲以上的人觀看。

> **說明**
>
> i.e. = (拉丁語) id est，意思是「即」、「換言之」(=that is; in other words)。將「i.e.」後面的詞彙用來解說「i.e.」前面的詞彙。

⓬ By so doing, it is hoped that Japan's government will save its increasingly burdened <u>pension</u> (i.e. <u>payment received after retirement</u>) system from going bankrupt.
藉由這樣做，希望日本政府會挽救日益不堪重負的養老金制度（即退休後收到的款項），使其免於破產。

考古題測驗與解析

Choose the answer that best completes each sentence below.

1. The beer market currently faces its fifth consecutive year of overall volume losses, **and** the sales of light beers have been consistently _____.

A dwindling　　**B** expanding　　**C** manipulating　　**D** speculating

中譯	啤酒市場正面臨連續第五年的整體銷售量虧損，淡啤酒的銷售一直在持續減少。 **A**（逐漸）減少、縮減　　**B** 擴大、增加 **C**（暗中）控制、操縱　　**D** 推測；猜測
取樣	瀏覽全文，藉標示詞and猜測前後句語意呈現並列，前後句負向的意義必須一致，取樣前句的名詞片語overall volume losses（整體銷售量虧損）。
預測	空格內應填入和overall volume lossess語意緊密且負向的字詞，依常理推斷，啤酒市場正面臨連續第五年的整體銷售量虧損，淡啤酒的銷量也會隨之減少，預測選項 **A** dwindling（（逐漸）減少、縮減）為可能答案。
檢驗	將 **A** 選項填入空格中檢驗句意。
確認	瀏覽上下句，整體句意連貫，確認答案為 **A**，正確答案就在題目上。

2. Plastic bags are not _____, **that is**, decades after they are buried in a landfill, they become nothing but still plastic bags.

A combustible　　**B** reusable　　**C** biodegradable　　**D** transferable

中譯	塑膠袋不可生物分解，也就是說，埋在垃圾場數十年後，它們仍然還是塑膠袋。 **A** 可燃的；易燃的　　**B** 可重複使用的 **C**（廢紙、飯屑等）可生物分解的 **D** 可轉移的；可調動的

取樣	瀏覽全文，從解釋性的片語that is（也就是說；換句話說）可知後句解釋前句，有助於讀者挑選正確答案，取樣後句的名詞片語nothing but still plastic bags（仍然只是塑膠袋）。此外，也取樣前句的否定詞not（不）。 **注意** nothing but的意思是「只、僅僅」。
預測	空格內應填入和nothing but still plastic bags語意緊密相關的字詞，按常理判斷，塑膠袋埋了數十年後仍然是塑膠袋，別無一物，表示其不可生物分解，因為題目中有否定詞not，預測選項 **C** biodegradable（可生物分解的）為可能答案。
檢驗	將 **C** 選項填入空格中檢驗句意。
確認	瀏覽上下句，整體句意連貫，確認答案為 **C**，正確答案就在題目上。有關否定關鍵詞，請參閱第13頁祕訣1。

3. A woman was stabbed to death in Queens, as 38 neighbors watched, doing nothing to alert the police. The news came to speak for urban _____ **and** moral decline **as well as** people's unwillingness to get involved.

A perturbation **B** pantheon **C** clamor **D** apathy

中譯	有三十八個鄰居目睹有名女子在皇后區遭人刺死，卻沒有任何人報警。這則新聞表現出城市的冷漠、道德的淪喪以及民眾不願被牽連在內。 **A** 煩亂　　**B**（一國或一個民族信仰的）眾神；（統稱某一領域的）名人、名流 **C** 大聲喊叫；喧鬧　　**D** 冷漠；缺乏情感
取樣	瀏覽全文，藉標示詞and猜測前後語意呈現負面並列關係，意義必須前因後果一致，取樣後面的名詞片語moral decline（道德淪喪）。此外，藉標示詞as well as（和）猜測前後語意呈現負面並列關係，意義必須前因後果一致，取樣後面的名詞片語people's unwillingness to get involved（民眾不願被牽連其中）。

預測	空格內應填入和負面線索moral decline以及people's unwillingness to get involved語意緊密相關的字詞，從生活經驗判斷，因為都市人冷漠，兼之道德淪喪，很多人遇到事情不願意伸手解圍，預測選項 **D** apathy（冷漠；淡漠）符合這個語境。
檢驗	將 **D** 選項填入空格中檢驗句意。
確認	瀏覽上下句，整體句意連貫，確認答案為 **D**，正確答案就在題目上。

4. The use of politically correct language is commonly seen as a friendly gesture to people outside our cultural groups. **In other words**, by using PC terms, we **not only** avoid _____ others, **but also** build mutual respect.

   A offending　　**B** attempting　　**C** attending　　**D** objecting

中譯	使用政治正確的語言通常被視為對我們文化群體外的人友善的表示。換句話說，藉著使用政治正確的術語，我們不僅避免冒犯他人，還建立了相互尊重。 **A** 得罪；冒犯　　**B** 企圖；試圖 **C** 出席；參加　　**D** 不贊成；反對
取樣	瀏覽全文，藉標示詞not only...but also（不但……而且……）猜測前後句語意呈現正向並列，正向意義必須一致，取樣後面正向的動詞片語build mutual respect（建立了相互尊重）和前面的動詞avoid（避免）。此外，瀏覽全文，從解釋性的片語In other words（換句話說）可知後句解釋前句，所以取樣前句的friendly (gesture)（友善的表示）。
預測	空格內應填入和build mutual respect、friendly語意緊密相關的字詞，build mutual respect、friendly都具有正向意涵，但因avoid後面要接負向含義的的字詞，這樣才會負負得正，not only後面所接的動詞片語才會呈現正向含義，預測選項 **A** offending（得罪；冒犯）符合這個語境。
檢驗	將 **A** 選項填入空格中檢驗句意。

| 確認 | 瀏覽上下句，整體句意連貫，確認答案為 Ⓐ，正確答案就在題目上。 |

5. Employees of this five-star hotel are trained to be not only respectful **and** _____, but also capable of dealing with any customers' complaints.

   Ⓐ haughty　　Ⓑ specious　　Ⓒ reactionary　　Ⓓ deferential

中譯	這家五星級飯店的員工接受培訓，不僅要表現尊重和恭敬，而且要能夠處理所有顧客的投訴。 Ⓐ 傲慢的；高傲自大的　　Ⓑ 似是而非的；貌似有理的 Ⓒ （於政治、思想等方面）反動的 Ⓓ 尊敬的、尊重的；順從的
取樣	瀏覽全文，藉標示詞 and 猜測前後句語意必須呈現並列（equality of ideas），前後正向的意義必須一致，取樣前面句有「正向」含義的形容詞 respectful（尊重的）。
預測	空格內應填入和 respectful 語意緊密相關的字詞，預測選項 Ⓓ deferential（尊敬的、尊重的）為可能答案。 respectful = deferential。
檢驗	將 Ⓓ 選項填入空格中檢驗句意。
確認	瀏覽上下句，整體句意連貫，確認答案為 Ⓓ，正確答案就在題目上。

6. The news about Lisa's secret engagement _____ quickly through Facebook**;** by the end of the day, all her colleagues had known about it.

   Ⓐ conjectured　　Ⓑ disseminated　　Ⓒ relinquished　　Ⓓ solicited

| 中譯 | 麗莎祕密訂婚的消息很快透過臉書傳開了；到了那天結束時，她所有的同事都知道了這件事。
Ⓐ 猜測；推測　　Ⓑ 散佈、傳播（訊息、知識、教義等）
Ⓒ （尤指不情願地）放棄
Ⓓ 索求、請求……給予（援助、錢或訊息） |

取樣	瀏覽全文，藉分號（;）猜測前後句意義必須呈現並列（equality of ideas），分號代替對等連接詞，連接兩個關係緊密的子句，取樣後句的all her colleagues had known（所有同事都知道）。
預測	空格內應填入和all her colleagues had known語意緊密相關的字詞，所有同事都知道麗莎祕密訂婚，代表消息已經傳開了，預測選項 **B** disseminated（散佈、傳播（訊息、知識等））符合這個語境。
檢驗	將 **B** 選項填入空格中檢驗句意。
確認	瀏覽上下句，整體句意連貫，確認答案為 **B**，正確答案就在題目上。

7. Surrounding the buildings are the rusted relics of the town's industrial past: ramshackle mining equipment, abandoned trailers, _____ trucks.

　A derelict　　**B** cerebral　　**C** doting　　**D** delusive

中譯	建築物的周圍是該城鎮過去工業活動所留下佈滿鐵鏽的遺跡：搖搖欲傾的採礦設備、被遺棄的拖車、<u>被棄置的</u>卡車。 **A** 被棄置的　　　　　**B** 大腦的；腦的 **C** 溺愛的；寵愛的　　**D** 不真實的；虛假的
文法解說	❶ 原句是The rusted...trucks are surrounding the building. 　　　　　　　S.（重）　　V.　分詞（片語）（輕） 為了讓「句子由輕到重」排列，句子成分所包含的字數愈多，其份量就愈重，愈重的句子成分愈要靠近句尾的位置出現。若要加強某一個句成分，成為訊息焦點，通常都會移到句尾的位置。因此把分詞片語提前，主詞與be動詞對調，形成倒裝句： Surrounding the building are the rusted...trucks. 　分詞（片語）（輕）　V.　　S.（重） 為什麼要將分詞片語提前（fronting）呢？ 第一，分詞提前目的是為了凸顯主詞（the rusted relics of the town's industrial past），主詞在句尾形成「句尾焦點」（end-focus），接著用冒號說明該城鎮過去工業活動所留下佈滿鐵鏽

文法解說	的遺跡，包含搖搖欲傾的採礦設備（ramshackle mining equipment）、被遺棄的拖車（abandoned trailers）、被棄的卡車（derelict trucks）。如果沒有將分詞片語提前，並將句子的主詞後置，主詞和冒號後的三個例子距離遙遠，句子的銜接性就沒有那麼好了。 第二，分詞提前的另一個目的是先營造背景（set the scene）或環境，使讀者或聽眾更容易理解或投入，通常包括提供相關的背景訊息、時間、地點等，以便引導讀者進入敘述中，最後才呈現句尾焦點，這種結構通常在新聞寫作中使用，目的是引起讀者的興趣，突出重要訊息。 Randolph Quirk，Sidney Greenbaum，Geoffrey Leech和Jan Svartvik所著的《英語綜合語法》（*A Comprehensive Grammar of the English Language*）也舉了幾例子在說明分詞提前，摘錄如下： Addressing the demonstration was a quite elderly woman. 　　　現在分詞（片語） 對示威群眾演講的是一位相當年長的婦人。 Shot by nationalist guerrillas were two entirely innocent tourists. 　　　過去分詞（片語） 遭民族主義游擊隊擊斃的是兩名完全無辜的遊客。 這兩個例子都在談論同一種句型結構：將述語中的分詞提前，並將主詞後置以凸顯主題，同時使用句子開頭部分的分詞片語來營造情境。第一個例子營造示威活動的背景，並凸顯參加者是一位相當年長的婦人，而第二個例子營造民族主義游擊隊擊斃人的背景，並凸顯受害者則是兩名完全無辜的遊客。 ❷ adj+N所組成的名詞片語，語意焦點在形容詞，請參閱第14頁祕訣3。
取樣	瀏覽全文，藉冒號（:）猜測前後句語意呈現負面並列，後面解釋前面，取樣前句的名詞片語rusted relics（佈滿鐵鏽的遺跡）。此外，透過逗號（,）猜測前後三個名詞片語語意呈現負面並列，因此取樣形容詞ramshackle（破爛不堪的）、abandoned（被遺棄的）。

預測	空格內應填入和rusted、ramshackle、abandoned語意緊密相關的字詞，根據題意，知道過去工業活動留下佈滿鐵鏽的遺跡，包括破爛不堪的採礦設備、被遺棄的拖車、破舊的卡車，預測選項 Ⓐ derelict（被棄置的）符合這個語境。
檢驗	將 Ⓐ 選項填入空格中檢驗句意。
確認	瀏覽上下句，整體句意連貫，確認答案為 Ⓐ，正確答案就在題目上。

8. Brevity is the soul of wit. In writing or delivering a public speech, we should avoid _____ ; **that is**, saying the same thing twice using different words.

Ⓐ oxymoron　　Ⓑ xenophobia　　Ⓒ tautology　　Ⓓ catharsis

中譯	簡潔是智慧之魂（言之簡潔為貴）。在寫作或發表公開演講時，我們應該避免贅述；也就是說，用不同的詞語重複說同一件事。 Ⓐ 矛盾修辭法、逆喻 Ⓑ 仇外、懼外（對外國人的厭惡或懼怕） Ⓒ 同義語的重複；贅述　　Ⓓ （使用瀉劑的）導瀉、通便
取樣	瀏覽全文，解釋性的片語 that is（也就是說；換句話說）是用來後面解釋前面要選的空格，所以取樣後句的動名詞片語 saying the same thing（說同一件事）和using different words（用不同的詞語）和動詞avoid（避免）。此外，藉句號（.）猜測前後句語意呈現並列，兩者緊密相關，後句解釋前句，取樣前句的名詞Brevity（簡潔）。
預測	空格內應填入和saying the same thing、using different words、Brevity語意緊密相關的字詞，簡潔就是避免贅述（用不同的詞語重複說同一件事），預測選項 Ⓒ tautology（同義反複；贅述）為可能答案。
檢驗	將 Ⓒ 選項填入空格中檢驗句意。

確認	瀏覽上下句，整體句意連貫，確認答案為 **C**，正確答案就在題目上。
單詞解釋	什麼是tautology呢？根據《牛津高階英漢雙解詞典》，tautology指的是「同義語的重複」、「贅述」。舉例來說，在「They spoke in turn, one after the other.」這句話中，in turn（輪流）和one after the other（依次地）表達相同的意思。這兩個副詞片語都是用來描述「他們輪流說話」這個概念，同時使用兩者會構成不必要的重複。為避免贅述，我們可以只保留片語中的一個，將句子簡化為「They spoke in turn.」或者「They spoke one after the other.」。這樣刪掉贅詞後的句子，讀起來才會簡潔有力。tautology用在邏輯學上，常翻譯為「套套邏輯」。

9. The actor was noted for his ＿＿＿＿＿ behavior: he quickly became irritated if his every whim was not immediately satisfied.

A mercenary　　**B** sedulous　　**C** vindictive　　**D** petulant

中譯	這位演員因其急躁的行為而聞名：如果他的每一個突發奇想沒有立即得到滿足，他就會很快變得惱火。 **A** 唯利是圖的、為金錢而工作的 **B** 勤勉的；孜孜不倦的 **C** 復仇心強的；報復的　　**D** 脾氣暴躁的；易怒的
取樣	瀏覽全文，藉冒號（:）猜測前後句語意呈現並列，後句解釋前句，取樣後句的動詞片語quickly became irritated（很快變得惱火）。但語意焦點在irritated，請參閱第13頁祕訣2。 **注意** 表「有名的」（noted）原因，介系詞用for而不是用because of，原因才是句意的焦點。
預測	空格內應填入和quickly became irritated語意緊密相關的字詞，依常理推斷，易惱火的人，其脾氣必定暴躁，預測選項 **D** petulant（易怒的；脾氣暴躁的）符合這個語境。
檢驗	將 **D** 選項填入空格中檢驗句意。

| 確認 | 瀏覽上下句，整體句意連貫，確認答案為 Ⓓ，正確答案就在題目上。 |

10. Simon earns a great fortune by trading in ＿＿＿＿＿. Those goods are all brought in secretly and illegally.

Ⓐ liaison　　Ⓑ nemesis　　Ⓒ dexterity　　Ⓓ contraband

中譯	西門靠交易走私貨品獲得了巨額財富。那些貨物都是偷偷非法進口的。 Ⓐ 聯絡；聯繫　　Ⓑ 報應；應得的懲罰 Ⓒ （手）靈巧、熟練；（思維）敏捷、靈活 Ⓓ （非法帶入或帶出國境的）禁運品、違禁走私品
取樣	瀏覽全文，藉句號（.）猜測前後句語意呈現負面並列，兩者緊密相關，後句解釋前句，取樣後句的被動動詞 brought in secretly and illegally（偷偷非法引口的）。
預測	空格內應填入和 brought in secretly and illegally 語意緊密且負面的字詞，依常理判斷，祕密非法引進的商品即走私貨，預測選項 Ⓓ contraband（（非法帶入或帶出國境的）禁運品、走私貨）為可能答案。
檢驗	將 Ⓓ 選項填入空格中檢驗句意。
確認	瀏覽上下句，整體句意連貫，確認答案為 Ⓓ，正確答案就在題目上。

11. To deal with ＿＿＿＿＿, the Japanese phone and car companies adopt some innovative approaches. **For example**, convenience stores offer safe havens for wandering pensioners with dementia.

Ⓐ clout　　Ⓑ publicity　　Ⓒ senility　　Ⓓ fortitude

中譯	為了對付老化問題，日本的電話和汽車公司採用了一些創新的方法。例如，便利商店為患有失智症的流浪退休老人提供了安全的庇護所。 Ⓐ 影響力；勢力　Ⓑ （媒體的）關注、宣傳 Ⓒ 衰老、老邁 Ⓓ （痛苦或困難面前表現出的）勇氣、膽量、剛毅
取樣	瀏覽全文，藉句點（.）猜測前後句語意呈現並列關係，此外，從舉例解釋時常用的詞語For example可知，後句說明前句，取樣後句的名詞片語wandering pensioners with dementia（患有失智症的流浪退休老人）。
預測	空格內應填入和wandering pensioners with dementia語意緊密相關的字詞，日本的電話和汽車公司為患有失智症的流浪退休人士提供了安全的庇護所，是針對老化問題所採取的創新方法，預測選項 Ⓒ senility（衰老、老邁）符合這個語境。
檢驗	將 Ⓒ 選項填入空格中檢驗句意。
確認	作者在對概念性的名詞如senility，一般會舉個隱喻「年老」概念的例子，如pensioner, dementia來幫助讀者理解提出的概念。瀏覽上下句，整體句意連貫，確認答案為 Ⓒ，正確答案就在題目上。

12. Health experts have warned that childhood obesity has been associated with a higher risk of obesity, _____ death **and** disability in adulthood.

　Ⓐ mundane　　Ⓑ vulnerable　　Ⓒ unprecedented　　Ⓓ premature

中譯	健康專家警告，童年肥胖與成年後肥胖、過早死亡和殘疾的較高風險有關。 Ⓐ 世俗的；世界的 Ⓑ （身體上或感情上）脆弱的、易受傷害的 Ⓒ 前所未有的；沒有先例的　　Ⓓ 未成熟的；過早的
取樣	瀏覽全文，藉標示詞and猜測前後語意呈現並列關係，意義必須相關或相稱，取樣名詞obesity（肥胖）、disability（殘疾、障礙）。

預測	空格內應填入和負面線索obesity、disability語意負向相關的字詞，從常理來推斷，童年肥胖與成年期肥胖、過早死亡和殘疾的較高風險有關，預測選項 **D** premature（未成熟的；過早的）符合這個語境。
檢驗	將 **D** 選項填入空格中檢驗句意。
確認	瀏覽上下句，整體句意連貫，確認答案為 **D**，正確答案就在題目上。

13. The three-time Academy Award winner's grace, skill and virtuosity completely _____ her audiences. They dared not speak nor breathe lest they missed anything in her performance.

A enthralled　　**B** convinced　　**C** authenticated　　**D** substantiated

中譯	三屆奧斯卡金像獎得主的優雅、技巧和精湛演技完全迷住了她的觀眾。他們不敢開口，也不敢呼吸，唯恐錯過表演中的任何細節。 **A** 使著迷；吸引住　　**B** 使確信；使信服 **C** 證明……是真實的　　**D** 證實；證明
取樣	瀏覽全文，藉由第一句的句點（.）猜測前後句意義必須呈現相等或相稱，後句補充說明前句，取樣後句的副詞子句lest they missed anything（唯恐錯過任何細節）。
預測	空格內應填入和lest they missed anything語意緊密相關的字詞，依常理推斷，看表演時觀眾們不敢錯過任一細節，表示表演精湛，令人著迷，預測選項 **A** enthralled（使著迷；吸引住）符合這個語境。
檢驗	將 **A** 選項填入空格中檢驗句意。
確認	瀏覽上下句，整體句意連貫，確認答案為 **A**，正確答案就在題目上。

14. Dolphins and sharks are natural enemies. Sharks are _____ of dolphins, and will kill and eat young dolphins if they can.

Ⓐ predators　　**Ⓑ** protectors　　**Ⓒ** successors　　**Ⓓ** survivors

中譯	海豚和鯊魚是自然界的天敵。鯊魚是海豚的掠食者，一有機會，就會殺害並吃掉年幼的海豚。 Ⓐ 掠奪者；捕食其他動物之動物　　Ⓑ 保護者；防禦者 Ⓒ 接替者；繼任者　　Ⓓ 生存者；倖存者
取樣	瀏覽全文，藉由第一句的句點（.）猜測前後句意義必須呈現相等或相稱，後句補充說明前句，取樣前句的名詞片語natural enemies（天敵）。
預測	空格內應填入和natural enemies語意緊密相關的字詞，預測選項Ⓐ predators（掠食者）符合這個語境。
檢驗	將 Ⓐ 選項填入空格中檢驗句意。
確認	瀏覽上下句，整體句意連貫，確認答案為 Ⓐ，正確答案就在題目上。

15. Upon hearing Joe's humorous remarks on the serious issue, the chairperson of the committee eyed him coldly, asking him to be scrupulous, not to be _____.

Ⓐ facetious　　**Ⓑ** decorous　　**Ⓒ** covetous　　**Ⓓ** rapacious

中譯	一聽到喬對嚴肅問題發表滑稽評論後，委員會主席就冷冷地瞪著他，要求他謹慎一點，不要亂開玩笑。 Ⓐ 好開玩笑的；滑稽的　　Ⓑ 有禮貌的；端莊穩重的 Ⓒ 貪求（他人之物）的；垂涎的　Ⓓ 貪婪的；強取的
取樣	瀏覽全文，藉由最後的逗點（,）猜測前後句意義必須呈現相等或相稱，後面補充說明前面，取樣前面的形容詞scrupulous（嚴謹的）。此外，也取樣否定詞not（不）。

預測	空格內應填入和scrupulous語意緊密且正向的形容詞，因為句中有否定詞not，須選和scrupulous語意相反的形容詞，使其負負得正，預測選項 Ⓐ facetious（亂開玩笑的）符合這個語境。 另外，其他值得一提的就是upon的用法。介系詞upon意思是「（在某事發生時）一……就」（相當於連接詞片語as soon as） 例 Upon his arrival home, he switched on the TV. ＝ As soon as he arrived home, he switched on the TV. 他一到家就打開電視。
檢驗	將 Ⓐ 選項填入空格中檢驗句意。
確認	瀏覽上下句，整體句意連貫，確認答案為 Ⓐ，正確答案就在題目上。注意，humorous與facetious幾乎是同義字。

16. People frequently overestimated their ability to communicate, **and this** was more _____ with people they knew well.

Ⓐ abominable　　Ⓑ pronounced　　Ⓒ sanguine　　Ⓓ obnoxious

中譯	一般人經常高估自己的溝通能力，這種現象在熟悉的人身上更加明顯。 Ⓐ 令人憎惡的；討厭的　　Ⓑ 顯著的；很明顯的 Ⓒ 充滿信心的；樂觀的　　Ⓓ 極討厭的；可憎的
取樣	瀏覽全文，藉標示詞and this猜測前後句語意呈現並列，意義必須一致或相稱，取樣前句的動詞片語frequently overestimated their ability to communicate（經常高估自己的溝通能力）。後句的this指的就是「經常高估自己的溝通能力」這件事。
預測	空格內應填入和frequently overestimated ability to communicate語意緊密相關的字詞，依常理推斷，會高估自己的溝通能力的人，面對自己熟悉的人往往溝通更順暢，更會高估自己的溝通能力，預測選項 Ⓑ pronounced（顯著的；很明顯的）為可能答案。
檢驗	將 Ⓑ 選項填入空格中檢驗句意。

| 確認 | 瀏覽上下句，整體句意連貫，確認答案為 **B**，正確答案就在題目上。 |

17. Overfishing is reaching _____ levels. According to a recent study, stocks of the biggest predatory species, such as tuna and swordfish, may have fallen by 90% since the 1950s.

   A egalitarian　　**B** concluding　　**C** catastrophic　　**D** soothing

中譯	過度捕撈快要達到災難性的程度。根據最近的研究，自上世紀50年代以來，最大型的掠食性魚類（例如金槍魚和劍魚）的數量可能已減少了90%。 **A** 主張人人平等的；平等主義的 **B** （一系列事物中）最後的、結尾的、結局的 **C** 大災禍的、大災難的　　**D** 安慰的
取樣	瀏覽全文，藉由第一句的句點（.）猜測前後句意義必須呈現相等或相稱，後句補充說明前句，取樣後句的動詞片語may have fallen by 90%（可能已減少了90%）。
預測	空格內應填入和表「負面」結果may have fallen by 90%有關，且表「原因」的字詞，按常理推斷，最大型的掠食性魚類的數量可能已減少了90%，很可能是因為過度捕撈快要達災難性程度所致，預測選項 **C** catastrophic（大災禍的、大災難的）符合這個語境。
檢驗	將 **C** 選項填入空格中檢驗句意。
確認	瀏覽上下句，整體句意連貫，確認答案為 **C**，正確答案就在題目上。

18. When the little boy had a headache and there was no aspirin in the house, his mother gave him a/an _____ : a small candy that she told him was a "pain pill," and it worked because his headache went away.

   A tumult　　**B** antithesis　　**C** analogy　　**D** placebo

中譯	當小男孩頭痛而家裡沒有阿司匹林時，他的媽媽給了他<u>安慰劑</u>：一顆小糖果，她告訴小男孩這是一顆「止痛藥」，而它奏效了，因為他的頭痛消失了。 Ⓐ 混亂；騷動　　Ⓑ（二者間的）對比、正相反 Ⓒ 類比；比擬　　Ⓓ 安慰劑；寬心藥
取樣	瀏覽全文，藉冒號（:）猜測前後句語意呈現並列，後句解釋前句，取樣後句的名詞片語"pain pill"（止痛藥）。注意，這裡的引號是用以表示某些詞語的特殊含義，而不是字面上的意思，如果作者不使用引號，那麼句子的意思就會是小男孩吃了止痛藥，而且真的發揮止痛的作用。但作者使用引號，就讓讀者產生了疑問：媽媽給的真的是止痛藥嗎？還是安慰劑呢？安慰劑真的有止痛的效果嗎？作者的意思是，安慰劑的效果並不在於藥物的成分，而是在於患者的心理作用。請參閱第19頁祕訣10。
預測	空格內應填入和"pain pill"語意緊密相關的字詞，依常理推斷，媽媽給的糖果，被小男孩當成「止痛藥」，居然奏效了，很可能是小男孩的心理作用所致，預測選項 Ⓓ placebo（安慰劑）符合這個語境。
檢驗	將 Ⓓ 選項填入空格中檢驗句意。
確認	瀏覽上下句，整體句意連貫，確認答案為 Ⓓ，正確答案就在題目上。

19. George had decided to leave this company, but after talking to his boss who begged him to stay, he was stuck in a ＿＿＿＿＿—should he go or shouldn't he?

　　Ⓐ hierarchy　　Ⓑ travesty　　Ⓒ quandary　　Ⓓ platitude

中譯	喬治原本已決定離開這家公司，但和苦苦哀求他留下的老闆談過之後，他<u>猶豫不決</u>——是該離開還是留下？ Ⓐ 等級制度（尤指社會或組織）　Ⓑ 滑稽模仿；歪曲 Ⓒ 困惑；進退兩難；窘境　　　　Ⓓ 陳詞濫調；平凡

取樣	瀏覽全文，藉破折號（─）猜測前後語意呈現並列關係，破折號是舉例說明時常會用到的標點符號，後面補充說明前面，取樣後面的問句should he go or shouldn't he?（離開還是留下）。
預測	空格內應填入和should he go or shouldn't he?語意緊密相關的字詞，離開公司還是留下，已成兩難問題，預測選項 **C** quandary（進退兩難）符合這個語境。
檢驗	將 **C** 選項填入空格中檢驗句意。
確認	瀏覽上下句，整體句意連貫，確認答案為 **C**，正確答案就在題目上。quandary是一個生詞，一般考生不知道是什麼意思，但通過破折號後面的should he go or shouldn't he，考生就可以輕鬆地知道quandary是「左右為難；進退兩難」的意思。

20. To many beginners, the behavior of the stock market appears to be _____. They cannot predict its performance.

A eclectic　　**B** eligible　　**C** erratic　　**D** erudite　　**E** evocative

中譯	對於許多初學者來說，股市的運作似乎是反覆無常的。他們無法預測其表現。 **A** 折衷性的；自不同材料加以挑選的 **B** 有資格的；合格的　　**C** 不穩定的；反覆無常的 **D** 博學的；有學問的　　**E** 引起記憶的；喚起感情的
取樣	瀏覽全文，藉由第一句的句點（.）猜測前後句意義必須呈現相等或相稱，後句補充說明前句，取樣後句的否定動詞片語cannot predict（無法預測）。
預測	空格內應填入和cannot predict語意緊密相關的字詞，按常理推斷，對初學者來說股市運作變化無常，無法預測，預測選項 **C** erratic（反覆無常的；不穩定的）符合這個語境。
檢驗	將 **C** 選項填入空格中檢驗句意。
確認	瀏覽上下句，整體句意連貫，確認答案為 **C**，正確答案就在題目上。

21. British physician Thomas Percival, echoing the words of Francis Bacon, insisted that it was the physician's responsibility to"＿＿＿＿＿ despair, alleviate pain, and soothe mental anguish."

Ⓐ deviate　　**Ⓑ** bloviate　　**Ⓒ** obviate　　**Ⓓ** exuviate　　**Ⓔ** aviate

中譯	英國醫師湯瑪斯·珀西瓦爾，附和弗朗西斯·培根的話，堅稱醫生的責任是「<u>防止絕望、減輕痛苦、舒緩精神痛苦</u>」。 Ⓐ 逸出正軌；背離　　Ⓑ（空泛地）高談闊論；夸夸其談 Ⓒ 排除（障礙；危險等）；消除；（事前）防止；避免 Ⓓ 蛻（皮）；脫（殼）；脫落（羽毛） Ⓔ 飛行；駕駛（飛機）
取樣	瀏覽全文，藉由引號內的逗點（,）猜測前後意義必須呈現相等或相稱，取樣動詞alleviate（減輕）、soothe（緩解、緩和）。
預測	空格內應填入和alleviate、soothe語意正向相關的字詞，預測選項 Ⓒ obviate（事前防止）符合這個語境。obviate despair的意思是「防止絕望」。
檢驗	將 Ⓒ 選項填入空格中檢驗句意。
確認	瀏覽上下句，整體句意連貫，確認答案為 Ⓒ，正確答案就在題目上。

22. Doctors are frequently criticized for their lack of "humanity": interest in the symptom rather than the person, a ＿＿＿＿＿ manner and cultivated professional indifference to "difference".

Ⓐ caique　　**Ⓑ** brusque　　**Ⓒ** unique　　**Ⓓ** plaque　　**Ⓔ** torque

中譯	醫生經常因缺乏「人道關懷」而受到批評：他們對症狀而非對人感興趣，這是一種<u>獨特的</u>舉止和刻意培養出來的對「差異」的專業漠視。 Ⓐ（Bosporus海峽之）一種輕舟 Ⓑ（指語言或態度）粗暴的；唐突的 Ⓒ 獨特的；獨一無二的　　Ⓓ（紀念性的）牌匾；牙菌斑 Ⓔ（使機器等旋轉的）轉矩

取樣	瀏覽全文，藉冒號（:）猜測前後句語意呈現並列，後句解釋前句，取樣前句的名詞片語lack of "humanity"（缺乏「人道關懷」）。此外，也可以藉由逗號（,）後的同位語判斷逗點前後指的是同一件事，逗點後有空格，須從逗點前面找答案，取樣名詞interest in the symptom（對症狀感興趣）。 **注意** 表「獎勵（reward）、懲罰（punish）、「批評」（criticize）」的原因，介系詞要用for而不是用because of，「原因」才是句意的焦點。
預測	空格內應填入和lack of "humanity"、interest in the symptom語意緊密相關的字詞，有些醫生對於患者的症狀感興趣，對患者缺乏「人道關懷」，這是個獨特的舉止，預測選項 **❸** unique（獨特的；獨一無二的）符合這個語境。
檢驗	將 **❸** 選項填入空格中檢驗句意。
確認	瀏覽上下句，整體句意連貫，確認答案為 **❸**，正確答案就在題目上。

23. Genetic discoveries will trigger a flood of new _____, **including** drugs that aimed at the causes of disease rather than the symptoms.

Ⓐ therapies　　**Ⓑ** diagnoses　　**Ⓒ** stethoscopes　　**Ⓓ** pharmaceuticals

中譯	基因發現將觸發大量新藥物的出現，包括針對疾病原因而非症狀的藥物。 **Ⓐ** 治療　**Ⓑ** 診斷（疾病）　**Ⓒ** 聽診器　**Ⓓ** 藥物
取樣	瀏覽全文，藉舉例時常用的詞語，including（包括）所引導的後半部是用來解釋前面要挑選的空格，取樣後句的drugs（藥物）。drugs= pharmaceuticals。
預測	空格內應填入和drugs語意緊密相關的字詞，預測選項 **Ⓓ** pharmaceuticals（藥物）符合這個語境。
檢驗	將 **Ⓓ** 選項填入空格中檢驗句意。
確認	瀏覽上下句，整體句意連貫，確認答案為 **Ⓓ**，正確答案就在題目上。

24. The professor _____ his theory during the lecture **and** gave only a vague outline of his ideas, leaving the students confounded.

Ⓐ besmirched　　**Ⓑ** promulgated　　**Ⓒ** recapitulated　　**Ⓓ** adumbrated

中譯	教授在講課時概述了他的理論，只把他的想法給了一個模糊的輪廓，因此學生們感到很困惑。 Ⓐ 詆毀；糟蹋（名聲等）　　Ⓑ 頒佈；公佈（法令等） Ⓒ 重述；概括　　Ⓓ 暗示；輕描淡寫；打輪廓
取樣	瀏覽全文，藉標示詞and猜測前後語意呈現並列關係，意義必須相關或相稱，取樣動詞片語gave only a vague outline（給了一個模糊的輪廓）。
預測	空格內應填入和only a vague outline語意緊密相關的字詞，預測選項 Ⓓ adumbrated（暗示；輕描淡寫；打輪廓）符合這個語境。注意，adumbrated中的umber字根意思是「陰影；影子」，影子雖是實體的投射，但輪廓模糊，和vague outline有異曲同工之妙。至於only，請參閱第16頁祕訣7。那為什麼不選 Ⓒ 呢？從英文定義著手就可以知道兩字的差異，recapitulate的意思是「to give a summary of the main points；summarize」，而adumbrate的意思是「to indicate faintly; outline」，呼應題目中的a vague outline of his ideas，正確答案就在題目上。
檢驗	將 Ⓓ 選項填入空格中檢驗句意。
確認	瀏覽上下句，整體句意連貫，確認答案為 Ⓓ，正確答案就在題目上。

25. As a product manager his style is honest and sincere; free of business school _____, he simply demonstrates the strengths of the new product.

Ⓐ hedonism   Ⓑ hyperbole   Ⓒ idyll   Ⓓ imbroglio

中譯	作為產品經理，他的風格誠實真誠；沒有商學院的誇張之詞，他僅僅展示這項新產品的優點。 Ⓐ 享樂主義　Ⓑ （修飾）誇張法 Ⓒ 田園詩　　Ⓓ 紛亂；糾葛
取樣	瀏覽全文，藉分號（;）猜測前後句意義必須呈現正面並列（equality of ideas），分號代替對等連接詞，連接兩個關係緊密的子句，取樣前句的honest and sincere（誠實真誠）。此外，也取樣否定詞free of（=without 沒有……的）。
預測	空格內應填入和honest and sincere語意緊密相關的字詞，因為題目中出現free of（負），因此必須選和honest and sincere語意相反的字，預測選項 Ⓑ hyperbole（誇張）（負），負負得正，才能符合這個語境。請參閱第13頁祕訣1。
檢驗	將 Ⓑ 選項填入空格中檢驗句意。
確認	瀏覽上下句，整體句意連貫，確認答案為 Ⓑ，正確答案就在題目上。

實戰練習

1. Everyone was impressed with their dignity **and** _____ while they were in vigil for their late mother.

   Ⓐ hypothesis   **Ⓑ** wilderness   **Ⓒ** composure   **Ⓓ** registration

2. The director claims the new plan will save as much as $16 million a year in operating costs, **or** the _____ of adding 50 percent to the library system's endowment.

   Ⓐ value   **Ⓑ** revenue   **Ⓒ** equivalent   **Ⓓ** asset

3. Paradoxically, England's colonization of North America was _____ by its success: the increasing prosperity of the colonies diminished their dependence upon, and hence their loyalty to, their home country.

   Ⓐ overshadowed   **Ⓑ** intervened   **Ⓒ** altered   **Ⓓ** undermined

4. That poet had been regarded as a child prodigy because he could distinguish the meanings of similar words. Years later, he composed many exquisite poems by means of his _____ **and** endeavor.

   Ⓐ ingenuity   **Ⓑ** indignity   **Ⓒ** integrity   **Ⓓ** indignation
   Ⓔ interregnum

5. The symptoms of depression are easy to recognize: sadness, bouts of crying for no apparent reason, irritability, insomnia, lack of appetite, restlessness, boredom, lack of interest in sex, _____ about one's appearance, **and** a general malaise and decrease in energy.

   Ⓐ vertigo   **Ⓑ** fiasco   **Ⓒ** inertia   **Ⓓ** euphoria

6. A survey implies that decreases in media coverage requesting donations can also suppress our charitable impulses. **For instance**, the survey notes that contributions to aid refugees fleeing the Rwandan genocide seemed to _____ in 1994 when events there were eclipsed in the American press by coverage of the O.J. Simpson murder investigation.

   Ⓐ kick in   Ⓑ draw on   Ⓒ trail behind   Ⓓ tail off

   註 作者有修改本題語意不清之處。

7. Most parks have picnic tables, park benches, drinking fountains, and playground equipment **such as** swings, slides and monkey _____.

   Ⓐ nuts   Ⓑ suits   Ⓒ bars   Ⓓ puzzles

8. It is difficult to _____ the factors which contribute to the spread of the new virus. More extensive research is obviously required.

   Ⓐ distract   Ⓑ dispatch   Ⓒ disseminate   Ⓓ disentangle

9. Cognitive factors are highly _____ to mental and intellectual functions. Many studies have investigated what cognitive factors make learning successful.

   Ⓐ pertinent   Ⓑ prevalent   Ⓒ persistent   Ⓓ preeminent

10. A new study suggests that there seems to be a limit to human lifespan. However, the results, based on demographic data, are far from _____ **and** must be interpreted carefully.

    Ⓐ suggestive   Ⓑ conclusive   Ⓒ ambiguous   Ⓓ doubtful

實戰練習 143

11. She already tried emotional _____ (=tried to make him feel guilty) to stop him from leaving.

　　Ⓐ intelligence　Ⓑ quotient　Ⓒ difficulties　Ⓓ blackmail

　　註 作者有修改本題語意不清之處。

12. Smartphone _____ is everywhere. Take a glance at your day-to-day life and you'll notice your friends are a bit too preoccupied with their iOS or Android devices. Some even claim they can't live without their cell phone.

　　Ⓐ connection　Ⓑ dependency　Ⓒ delinquency　Ⓓ wave

解答

1. Ⓒ　2. Ⓒ　3. Ⓓ　4. Ⓐ　5. Ⓒ　6. Ⓓ　7. Ⓒ　8. Ⓓ　9. Ⓐ　10. Ⓑ
11. Ⓓ　12. Ⓑ

Chapter 5

認識修飾語結構：

MODIFIER 型

題型解說

Modifier 型【修飾語結構（句中帶有修飾語，如形容詞、副詞等）】

本章節要介紹的是 Modifier 型，這類型的句子帶有修飾語，如形容詞、副詞等。我們來看看修飾語的定義是什麼？

A modifier is a word, a phrase, or other sentence elements that describe, qualify, or limit another element in the same sentence.
修飾語是指一個詞、片語或其他句子成分，用來描述、限定或限制同一句子中的另一個成分。

做題時需要斟酌、考慮下列的修飾語：

- **Ⓐ** 同位語
- **Ⓑ** 分詞片語
- **Ⓒ** 主詞補語
- **Ⓓ** 形容詞
- **Ⓔ** 形容詞子句
- **Ⓕ** 關係副詞
- **Ⓖ** 介+名（形容詞片語）
- **Ⓗ** 副詞／副詞片語／副詞子句
- **Ⓘ** 表「比較」的副詞子句：比較要同類
- **Ⓙ** 八大類副詞子句
- **Ⓚ** 表「目的」的副詞子句

Ⓐ 同位語

❶ 同位語是由非限定形容詞子句轉變而成

轉變法則 參閱 147 頁例 1～例 3

Step 1：取消關係代名詞 who 或 which
Step 2：be 動詞省略

❷ 同位語的作用

　　同位語（appositive）通常附加在名詞之後，而指涉對象與前面的名詞同一人、同一物或同一事，其作用只是補充說明前面的名詞而已，讓讀者更清楚了解所補述的人、物、事。不能視為單獨構句，也不能做該句的主題或主要觀念。其基本句型是「...N, 同位語 ,...」。此外，主詞（或受詞）和同位語之間常用逗號分開。

An appositive is a word or phrase that explains, identifies, or renames the word it follows. An appositive may be a noun phrase (that is, a noun and its modifiers.)

同位語是一個用來解釋、識別或重新命名其前的詞或片語。同位語可以是一個名詞片語（也就是一個名詞及其修飾詞）。

例1

<u>Mr. Smith</u>, our English teacher, is very knowledgeable.
　　　S

我們的英文老師史密斯先生學識淵博。　▶ 主格同位語

例2

We respect <u>Mr. Smith</u>, our English teacher, is very knowledgeable.
　　　　　　　O

我們尊敬我們的英文老師史密斯先生。　▶ 受格同位語

例3

Dr. Sun Yat-sen, (who is) <u>the National Father of the Republic of China</u>, is a great man.　　　　　　　(noun phrase)

中華民國國父孫中山先生是偉人。

例 4

Robert Peary, an _____ explorer, was the first to reach the North Pole.

ⓐ insipid ⓑ petrified ⓒ intrepid ⓓ apprehensive

羅伯特皮爾里是第一位到達北極的<u>勇敢</u>探險家。　　　答案：C

例 5

Mathematics, (which was) <u>once my favorite subject</u>, no longer interests me.
　　　　　　　　　　　　(noun phrase)

→ <u>Once my favorite subject</u>, **mathematics** no longer interests me.

▶ 同位語移位至句首(pre-posing)
曾經是我最喜歡的科目數學，現在已經不再吸引我了。

例 6

Lucy, (who is) <u>their eldest daughter</u>, is finishing high school this year.
　　　　　　　　(noun phrase)

→ <u>Their eldest daughter</u>, **Lucy** is finishing high school this year.

▶ 同位語移位至句首(pre-posing)
他們的長女露西今年即將完成高中學業。

例 7

In winter, we often have <u>dry and itchy skin,</u> a problem which can
　　　　　　　　　　　　　　　O

be treated by applying lotions or creams.

冬天時，我們常常有乾癢肌膚問題，這個問題可以用塗抹乳液或乳霜來治療。

B 分詞片語

❶ 出現在句首的分詞片語是由副詞子句簡化而成

$$\text{Ving} \,/\, \text{Vpp}..., \quad \text{S} + \text{V}$$
分詞片語　　　　主要子句

▶ 先從後主，加上逗號

❷ 符合以下兩個條件的副詞子句可簡化成分詞片語

條件 1：表時間、條件、原因的副詞子句

注意 在統測、學測、指考、教甄、高考考題裡，句首的分詞片語的句意幾乎都是表「原因」

條件 2：副詞子句中的主詞與主要子句中的主詞相同

❸ 簡化法則

Step 1：取消副詞子句中的連接詞

Step 2：主詞省略

Step 3：主動動詞改現在分詞，被動動詞改過去分詞

❹ 動詞改成分詞的形式

a) 主動簡單式：V → Ving

b) 主動完成式：has / have + Vpp → having + Vpp

c) 被動簡單式：be + Vpp → (being) + Vpp

d) 被動完成式：

has / have + been + Vpp → (havig + been) + Vpp

e) be 動詞：

$$\text{be} + \begin{cases} (\text{Adv.}) + \text{Adj.} \\ (\text{Adj.}) + \text{N} \end{cases} \rightarrow (\text{being}) \begin{cases} (\text{Adv.}) + \text{Adj.} \\ (\text{Adj.}) + \text{N} \end{cases}$$

注意 小括弧中的字可以省略，有時分詞片語中沒出現分詞，只見形容詞或名詞，那是因為being被省略了。

例1 Because John is seriously ill, he can't go to school.

→ (Being) **seriously ill**, John can't go to school.

約翰病得很嚴重,無法上學。

例2 Because he was influenced by his young friends, the boy dropped out of school for a while.

→ (Being) **influenced by his young friends**, the boy dropped out of school for a while.

這個男孩受到青少年朋友的影響,曾經輟學一段時間。

例3 Tired of the _____ of workday life, Jason took a gap year off and went on a solitary global expedition.

A subterfuge　**B** ubiquity　**C** chrysalis　**D** banality

因傑森厭倦了單調乏味的上班生活,他休了一年假,展開了獨自的全球探險之旅。

答案:D

❺ 主動改現在分詞、被動改過去分詞

為了句子簡潔有力,主從分明,第二個動詞如表次要動作,主動改成現在分詞,被動改成過去分詞,然後連接詞 and 用逗號(,)來取代。

例1

John stood there, waiting (=and waited) for his sister.
　　　　V1　　　　　　　　V2

約翰站在那裡等著他的妹妹。

例2

John wrote to his father, begging (=and begged)) .
　　　　V1　　　　　　　　　　V2

him to call on Prof. Smith

約翰寫信給他的父親,請他去拜訪史密斯教授。

150　Chapter 5 認識修飾語結構:MODIFIER 型

例3 We <u>passed</u> the evening very pleasantly, <u>eating</u> (=and ate)
　　　　　　V1　　　　　　　　　　　　　　　　　　V2
cookies and <u>playing</u> (=and played) the guitar.
　　　　　　　V3

我們愉快地度過了這個晚上，一邊吃餅，一邊彈吉他。

C 主詞補語

形容詞或名詞作主詞補語時，閱讀的重點應落在主詞補語上。

$$S + be + \begin{cases} (Adv.) + Adj. \\ (Adj.) + Noun \end{cases}$$

　　　　　　　(Subjective complement)

例1 A(n) _____ is someone from a low social class who has become rich or important; however this person is not accepted as an equal by other rich or important people because he/she is recognized as tawdry.

　Ⓐ sycophant　Ⓑ nonchalant　Ⓒ charlatan　Ⓓ parvenu

暴發戶是指出身低微但後來致富或取得重要地位者；然而，此人並不為其他富人或舉足輕重的人視為是同一層次的人，因為他們認為暴發戶是俗氣的。　　　　　　　　　　　答案：D

例2 Besides drugs, the concern and support of patients' families and friends as well as social acceptance are also a _____ for mental patients.

　Ⓐ vendetta　Ⓑ paragon　Ⓒ panacea　Ⓓ genesis

除了藥物之外，患者親朋好友的關心支持和社會接納也是精神病患者的靈丹妙藥。　　　　　　　　　　　　　　答案：C

Ⓓ 形容詞

形容詞通常放在名詞前面修飾名詞，因此語意上形容詞要比名詞重要。

$$\boxed{\text{Adj}} + \text{N}$$

Ⓔ 形容詞子句

❶ 關係代名詞（who、which、that）引導的形容詞子句要放在修飾的名詞後面。

N ＋ <u>關代 ＋ V</u>　▶主格關代
　　　(Adj. clause)

N ＋ <u>關代 ＋ S ＋ V</u>　▶受格關代
　　　(Adj. clause)

例1 I like those **girls** <u>who (主格) have inner beauty</u>.
我喜歡那些擁有內在美的女孩。

例2 This is the only **paper** <u>that (主格) contains the news</u>.
這是唯一的一份含有那則新聞的報紙。

例3 The **boy** <u>whom (受格) you saw yesterday</u> is his brother.
你昨天見過的男孩子是他的哥哥。

❷ 此外，限定用的形容詞子句可簡化為分詞片語，簡化後的分詞片語，仍放在名詞後面修飾。

簡化法則

Step 1：取消關係代名詞
Step 2：其後動詞若主動，改現在分詞
　　　　　其後動詞若被動，改過去分詞
Step 3：動詞若為 be 動詞，省略

例1 The boy <u>who speaks English</u> is his brother.

→ The boy **speaking English** is his brother.

會說英文的男孩是他的弟弟。

例2 A page <u>which is digested</u> is better than a volume <u>which is hurriedly read</u>.

→ A page **digested** is better than a volume **hurriedly read**.
　　　(word)　　　　　　　　　　　　　(phrase)

理解消化一頁勝過匆忙閱讀一整卷。

F 關係副詞

關係副詞（relative adverbs）也可引導形容詞子句，放在所修飾的名詞後面。主要的關係副詞有四個：when（表時間）、where（表地方）、why（表理由）、how（表方法）。此外，關係副詞前的先行詞為了避免和關係副詞「語意重複」，是可以省略的。

例1 Do you know (the time) <u>when she will arrive</u>?
　　　　　　　　　　　　　　▶ 修飾the time

你知不知道她到達的時間？

例2 Is this (the place) <u>where he was born</u>? ▶ 修飾the place

這裡是他出生的地方嗎？

例3 Information overload is inevitable in the modern society where _____ access to the world wide web is no longer an ideal but a status quo.

Ⓐ ludicrous　Ⓑ strident　Ⓒ transient　Ⓓ ubiquitous

在現代社會中，資訊過載已經不可避免的，能夠**隨處**存取全球資訊網已經不再是一種理想，而是一個現狀。　　答案：D

例4 John knows (the reason) <u>why she did it</u>.

約翰知道她為何做這個。　▶ 修飾the reason

> **說明**
>
> 為了避免「語意重複」，關係副詞 why 通常可以沒有先行詞 the reason，另外有時也可以省略 why，例如：The reason (why) <u>he didn't come</u> is unknown.

例5 Winning international fame, however, was neither the original intention nor the main reason <u>why Camake founded the group in 2006</u>. ▶ 修飾the reason

然而，贏得國際聲譽既不是最初意圖，也不是查馬克在2006年創立該團體的主要原因。

例6 No one knows <u>how he found it</u>.
沒人知道他是怎麼找到的。

> **說明**
>
> Michael Swan 在《牛津英語用法指南》一書中提到 the way 和 how 不能同時使用，因 way 的意思是「方法、手段」，而 how 的意思也是「（方法、手段）怎樣、如何」，只能擇一使用。除了「語意重複」的緣故，從詞性的觀點來看，the way 本身就可以當副詞，有別於 the time、the place、the reason 這些片語只能當名詞使用，要加上介系詞，形成 at the time、at the place、for the reason 才能當副詞使用。既然 the way 和 how 都可以當副詞，為求簡潔，所以擇一使用。例 6 除了寫成 No one knows how he found it. 也可寫成 No one knows the way he found it. 黃宋賢在《超越英文法》一書中舉了底下四個句子來說明為什麼不能用 the way how...。
>
> ❶ He did it **at** this time.
> 他在這個時候做了這件事。
>
> ❷ He did it **at** this place.
> 他在這個地方做了這件事。

❸ He did it **for** this reason.
他為了這個原因做了這件事。

❹ He did it (**in**) this way.
他用這個方法做了這件事。

從上述四句得知，this way 可以當副詞使用，而 this time、this place、this reason 必須加上介系詞才能當副詞使用，this way 和其他三者的詞性有差異。因為 the way how 的 the way 和 how 都是副詞，不須重複使用。

例7 Colors have a direct and powerful impact on the way we feel and react to our surroundings.
顏色對我們的感受和對周圍環境的回應方式具有直接而強大的影響。

例8 Europe's new measures should eventually both reduce the number of animals used in experiments and improve the way in which scientific research is conducted.
歐洲的新措施最終應該能減少實驗用的動物數量，並改善科學研究進行的方式。

說明

the way 和 how 不能同時使用，除了省略 how，也可以將 how 換成 in which 或 that，例如例 8 可以改寫為：Europe's new measures should eventually both reduce the number of animals used in experiments and improve the way (that) scientific research is conducted.

例9 Bol is also most proud of the way Little Free Library is bringing communities together.
波爾也非常自豪「小型免費圖書館」能讓社區凝聚在一起的方式。

Ⓖ 介+名（形容詞片語）

介系詞引導的形容詞片語要放在修飾的名詞後面。

$$N1 + 介 + N2 \text{ (形容詞片語)}$$

例1 The **book** on the desk is very interesting.
　　　桌上的書非常有趣。

例2 A **bird** in the hand is worth **two** in the bush.
　　　一鳥在手勝於兩鳥在林。→喻到手的東西才是可靠的。

Ⓗ 副詞／副詞片語／副詞子句

修飾動詞或形容詞，可用副詞（adverb）、副詞片語（adverbial phrase）或副詞子句（adverb clause）。副詞放置的位置相當有彈性，但通常放在動詞之後。副詞可分為：

❶ 時間副詞
❷ 頻率副詞
❸ 狀態副詞
❹ 地方副詞

Ⓘ 表「比較」的副詞子句：比較要同類

❶ 原級

$$S1 + \begin{Bmatrix} Be \\ V \end{Bmatrix} + \underline{as} + \begin{Bmatrix} Adj. \\ Adv. \end{Bmatrix} + \underline{as} + S2 + \begin{Bmatrix} Be \\ V \end{Bmatrix}$$
$$\qquad\qquad\qquad\qquad\text{adv.}\qquad\qquad\text{conj.}$$

▶ S1、S2要同類才可比較

例1 He talked <u>as</u> slowly <u>as</u> he could.
他盡可能緩慢地說話。

例2 This flower is <u>as</u> beautiful <u>as</u> the other one.
這朵花跟另一朵花一樣漂亮。

❷ 比較級
兩者間的比較用「比較級形容詞或副詞 + than」。

$$S1 + V + \begin{Bmatrix} \sim er \\ more\sim \end{Bmatrix} + than + S2 + V$$

▶ S1和S2要同類

例1 My mother is <u>taller than</u> I.
母親長得比我高。

例2 This book is <u>more interesting than</u> that one.
這本書比那本有趣。

Ⓙ 八大類副詞子句

種類	用法	例句	說明
副詞子句	表時間	❶His father died <u>when he was ten years old</u>. 他父親在他十歲的時候過世了。	副詞子句是用以修飾動詞、形容詞或其他副詞，如左。
	表條件	❷ <u>If it is fine</u>, we will go hiking. 天氣好的話，我們就去郊遊。 ▶ 連接詞if在中文裡不一定要翻譯成「假如、如果」	
	表理由、原因	❸ We are glad <u>because he is with us</u>. 我們很高興，因他與我們在一起。	

種類	用法	例句	說明
副詞子句	表地方	❹ <u>Where there is a will</u>, there is a way. 有志者事竟成。	副詞子句是用以修飾動詞、形容詞或其他副詞，如左。
	表目的	❺ We got up early <u>in order that we might catch the first train</u>. 我們早起是為了趕上第一班火車。	
	表結果	❻ John is so honest <u>that we all like him</u>. 約翰很誠實，所以我們都很喜歡他。	
	表讓步	❼ <u>Although it was raining</u>, we went out. 雖然在下雨，我們還是出門了。	
	表比較	❽ He is as rich <u>as you are</u>. 他跟你一樣富有。	

說明

副詞子句是用以修飾動詞、形容詞或其他副詞，如157~158頁例句。

❸ We are glad <u>because he is with us</u>. ▶ 修飾形容詞 glad

我們很高興，因他與我們在一起。

❻ John is so honest <u>that we all like him</u>. ▶ 修飾副詞 so

約翰很誠實，所以我們都很喜歡他。

❽ He is as rich <u>as you are</u>. ▶ 修飾副詞 as

他跟你一樣富有。

除❸、❻、❽外，其他例句的副詞子句都修飾動詞。

K 表「目的」的副詞子句

❶ 表「目的」的副詞子句，意思是為「為了、以便」，通常用 so that、in order that 或單獨用 that 引導，其中助動詞用 may 或 can，動詞過去式用 might 或 could。

例

Children go to school $\begin{Bmatrix} \text{that} \\ \text{so that} \\ \text{in order that} \end{Bmatrix}$ they may learn.

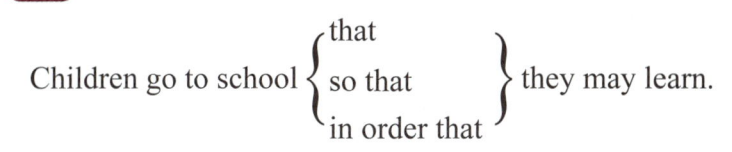

❷ 表目的的副詞子句或副詞片語放在主要子句的前面，通常用 in order that、in order to + V 或 to + V。

例1 <u>In order that children may learn</u>, they go to school.
<u>In order to learn</u>, children go to school.
小孩子為了學習都去上學。

例2 <u>To provide a nonsmoking environment</u>, many restaurants do not allow smoking inside.
為提供一個無菸的用餐環境，許多餐廳不允許室內抽菸。

上下文中的線索

英語學習者是否能依據上下文推測出生詞的含義，取決於是否能找出文章中的詞彙或句構所提供常見的線索來幫助理解，而非只靠生詞或單字本身的意思，應以整句或整段的理解為主。

「同義字／近義字」的線索（synonym or near-synonym clue）

為使前後兩句語意連貫，取樣詞義相同或相近的字詞，提供進一

步的訊息，進而推測生詞的意思。平時閱讀句子時，也應注意聯繫動詞（linking verbs），像是 be 動詞，因為此類動詞本身意思不完整，其後須加主詞補語（subjective complement），來補足句子主詞的意義。

❶ This tour package is very appealing, and that one is equally attractive. I don't know which one to choose.
這個套裝行程非常吸引人，而那個同樣有吸引力。我不知道該選擇哪一個。

❷ Hyperactive children always seem to be restless.
過動的孩子總是似乎無法安靜下來。

❸ An honest person is faithful to his promise. Once he makes a commitment, he will not go back on his own word.
誠實的人會忠於他的承諾。一旦他作出承諾，就不會食言。

❹ Irene does not throw away used envelopes. She recycles them by using them for taking telephone messages.
艾琳沒有丟棄用過的信封。她將信封回收再利用，用來記錄電話留言。

「同位語」的線索（appositive clue）

同位語（appositive）通常附加在名詞之後，而指涉對象與前面的名詞同一人、同一物或同一事，其作用只是補充說明前面較艱深的名詞（如例句❶專有名詞 Robert Peary），因此英語學習者可依據同位語推測生詞的含義。

❶ Robert Peary, an intrepid explorer, was the first to reach the North Pole.
羅伯特皮爾里是第一位到達北極的勇敢探險家。

> **說明**
>
> 他當時一定不知畏懼，才敢下決心走上探險北極之路。句子裡的 an intrepid explorer=Robert Peary 指同一人，有說明主詞的功能，所以是同位語。

❷ In winter, we often have dry and _____ skin, **a problem which is usually treated by applying lotions or creams**.

   Ⓐ alert   Ⓑ itchy   Ⓒ steady   Ⓓ flexible

中譯	冬天時，我們常常有乾癢肌膚問題，這個情況通常以塗抹乳液或乳霜來治療。 Ⓐ 警醒的　Ⓑ 癢的　Ⓒ 穩定的　Ⓓ 彈性的
文法解說	冠詞分三類： 有定冠詞 (definite) 用 the 表示　Ⓐ 有定 (definite)：意指說話人與聽話人皆知談何人、何事、何物 無定冠詞 (indefinite) 分二類，都用 a(an) 來表示　Ⓑ 有指 (specific)：說話人知但聽話人不知何人、何事、何物 　Ⓒ 無指 (nonspecific)：雙方（說話人、聽話人）都不知談何人、何事、何物 在此句的 a problem 的 a 是有指冠詞，所以只有說話人／出題者（說這句話的人）知，但考生、讀者不知，所以會問 What is the problem?（「什麼問題？」或「問題指什麼、指誰？」）問題（補充說明前面）是指「肌膚乾癢」，由於是指同一事，兩邊可以畫等號，所以是同位語，如圖示表示如下： N, =(a) N　▶ 指同一人、同一事、同一物
取樣	瀏覽全文，藉名詞片語 a problem 所引導的同位語判斷 a problem 即 dry and _____ skin。此外，which 所引導的限定形容詞子句提供必要的資訊來說明 a problem 代表什麼。解題關鍵在於修飾語，因此取樣被動動詞 is usually treated by applying lotions or creams（通常以塗抹乳液或乳霜來治療）。此外，也取樣名詞片語 dry and _____ skin。

預測	空格內應填入和 is usually treated by applying lotions or creams、dry and _____ skin 語意緊密相關的字詞。既然空格內應填入和 dry 語意緊密相關的形容詞，依生活經驗判斷，冬季皮膚常會乾癢，這樣的情況通常以塗抹乳液或乳霜來治療，預測選項 **B** itchy（癢的）為可能答案。
檢驗	將 **B** 選項填入空格中檢驗句意。
確認	瀏覽上下句，整體句意連貫，確認答案為 **B**。本題的題型是考修飾語：同位語、形容詞子句修飾名詞。

❸ **Spending most of his childhood in Spain**, John, **a native speaker of English**, is also _____ in Spanish.

Ⓐ promising　　**Ⓑ** grateful　　**Ⓒ** fluent　　**Ⓓ** definite

中譯	因為約翰在西班牙度過他童年大部分的時光，儘管他以英語為母語，但他也能說一口流利的西班牙語。 **Ⓐ** 有希望的；有前途的　　**Ⓑ** 感激的；表示感謝的 **Ⓒ** （尤指外語）流利的、文字流暢的　　**Ⓓ** 肯定的；確定的
取樣	瀏覽全文，同位語 a native speaker of English（以英語為母語的人）通常附加在名詞之後，補充說明前面的專有名詞 John（約翰）。解題關鍵在於修飾語，因此取樣同位語 a native speaker of English。此外，現在分詞片語 Spending most of his childhood in Spain 是由表示「原因」的副詞子句 Because John spent most of his childhood in Spain 省略而來的，用以修飾主要子句中的主詞 John，因為表「結果」的主要子句挖空，因此取樣表示「原因」的修飾語 Spending most of his childhood in Spain（在西班牙度過他童年大部分的時光）。
預測	因表「因果」關係，空格內應填入和 Spending most of his childhood in Spain 和 a native speaker of English 語意因果相關的字詞。依常理來推斷，約翰身為英語母語人士，英語應該講得流利，但因為約翰大部分的童年時光是在西班牙度過，西班牙語「也」（also）該和英語講得一樣流利，預測選項 **Ⓒ** fluent（（尤指外語）流利的）為可能答案。

檢驗	將 ❻ 選項填入空格中檢驗句意。
確認	瀏覽上下句，整體句意連貫，確認答案為 ❻。本題的題型是考修飾語：同位語、表「原因」的現在分詞片語修飾主詞。

「重述」的線索（restatement clue）

　　重述的線索很像同義字或近義字線索，但不同在於用字，重述的用字是用清晰易懂的字或片語去描述或解釋前面艱深難懂的字或片語，其前常用破折號（dash）或逗號（comma）或對等連接詞 and 或 or 與艱深難懂的字或片語相隔開。例如：

❶ Mike arrived at the meeting punctually at ten o'clock—as it was scheduled—not a minute early or late.
邁克按預定時間準時於十點抵達會場，一分都不差。

❷ If you want to keep your computer from being attacked by new viruses, you need to constantly renew and update your anti-virus software.
你若想讓你的電腦免受新病毒的侵襲，就須不斷更新你的防毒軟體。

❸ Howler monkeys are named for the long loud cries, or howls, that they make every day.
吼猴是因為牠們每天都發出長而響亮的叫聲，或吼聲得名。

❹ Students were asked to revise or rewrite their compositions based on the teacher's comments.
老師要求學生按照他的評語來修正或改寫作文。

❺ Microscopes are used in medical research labs for studying bacteria or germs that are too small to be visible to the naked eye.
顯微鏡在醫學實驗室裡被用來研究太小而無法被肉眼所看見的細菌或病菌。

考古題測驗與解析

Choose the answer that best completes each sentence below.

1. A jailed dissident prisoner returned home **under an _____ of the government.**

Ⓐ adjournment　　**Ⓑ** promontory　　**Ⓒ** amnesty　　**Ⓓ** accessory

中譯	一位被囚禁的異議人士獲得政府的特赦回家了。 Ⓐ 延期開會、休會　　Ⓑ 海岬、岬角 Ⓒ （對政治犯的）赦免、大赦　　Ⓓ 附件；配件
取樣	瀏覽全文，表「根據、按照」的介系詞under所引導的副詞片語修飾主要子句的動詞片語returned home（回家）。解題關鍵在於修飾語，但修飾語挖空，因此取樣被修飾語returned home。此外，也取樣prisoner（囚犯）的修飾語jailed dissident（被囚禁的異議份子）。注意：adj. + N所組成的名詞片語，語意焦點在形容詞，參閱第14頁祕訣3。
預測	空格內應填入和returned home、jailed dissident語意緊密相關的字詞，依常理推斷，被囚禁的異議份子，必須是服役期滿、保外就醫，或者政府特赦等因素才能出獄回家，預測選項 Ⓒ amnesty（（對政治犯的）赦免、大赦）符合這個語境。
檢驗	將 Ⓒ 選項填入空格中檢驗句意。
確認	瀏覽上下句，整體句意連貫，確認答案為Ⓒ，正確答案就在題目上。本題的題型是考修飾語：介系詞under所引導的副詞片語修飾主要子句的動詞。

2. India, having practiced the caste system for centuries, is usually perceived as a(n) _____ society, **in which individuals are ranked according to their wealth and power.**

   Ⓐ apathetic   Ⓑ hierarchical   Ⓒ juridical   Ⓓ sovereign

中譯	印度實行種姓制度長達數個世紀之久，印度通常被認為是一個階級分明的社會，這個社會是根據個人所擁有的財富和權力來排名。 Ⓐ 缺乏感情的、冷漠的　　Ⓑ 階級組織的、階層的 Ⓒ 司法上的；審判上的　　Ⓓ 有主權的；完全獨立的
取樣	瀏覽全文，in which(=where)所引導的非限定形容詞子句, in which individuals are ranked according to their wealth and power（這個社會是根據個人所擁有的財富和權力來排名）修飾前面主要子句中的先行詞society（社會）。解題關鍵在於修飾語，因此取樣被動動詞片語are ranked according to their wealth and power。此外，分詞片語, having practiced the caste system for centuries（實行種姓制度長達數個世紀之久）是從形容詞子句, which has practiced the caste system for centuries簡化而成，修飾India（印度），而India通常被認為是a(n) ___ society。解題關鍵在於修飾語，因此取樣修飾語中的名詞片語the caste system（種姓制度）。
預測	空格內應填入和are ranked according to their wealth and power、caste system語意緊密相關的形容詞，根據歷史常識來判斷，印度的種姓制度形成階級分明的社會，根據個人所擁有的財富和權力來排名，預測選項 Ⓑ hierarchical（階級組織的、階層的）符合這個語境。
檢驗	將 Ⓑ 選項填入空格中檢驗句意。
確認	瀏覽上下句，整體句意連貫，確認答案為 Ⓑ，正確答案就在題目上。本題的題型是考修飾語：in which所引導的形容詞子句修飾名詞、分詞片語修飾主詞。

3. Clothes oftentimes reflect society's values. For instance, in Victorian times, **when women were expected to be _____**, they wore clothing **that limited their movements**.

Ⓐ prolific　**Ⓑ** inactive　**Ⓒ** energetic　**Ⓓ** suggestive

中譯	服裝常常反映社會的價值觀。例如，維多利亞時代的社會期望女性要<u>不活動</u>，他們就穿著限制他們活動的服裝。 Ⓐ 多產的；創作豐富的　　Ⓑ 不活動的；不活潑的 Ⓒ 精力充沛的；充滿活力的　Ⓓ 暗示性的
取樣	瀏覽全文，表「時間」的從屬連接詞when所引導的副詞子句修飾後方主要子句動詞片語wore clothing（穿服裝），但修飾語挖空，必須從主要子句找線索。主要子句中的形容詞子句that limited their movements（限制他們活動的服裝）修飾先行詞clothing。解題關鍵在於修飾語，因此取樣修飾語中的動詞片語limited their movements。
預測	空格內應填入和limited their movements語意緊密相關的形容詞，從常理推斷，維多利亞社會期待女性要不活動，因此女性為了符合社會期待，會穿限制他們活動的服裝，預測選項 Ⓑ inactive（不活動的）符合這個語境。
檢驗	將 Ⓑ 選項填入空格中檢驗句意。
確認	瀏覽上下句，整體句意連貫，確認答案為 Ⓑ，正確答案就在題目上。本題的題型是考修飾語：when所引導的副詞子句修飾動詞片語、形容詞子句修飾先行詞。

4. The experienced pilot had to quickly _____ the helicopter to the right **in order to avoid colliding with the bird flying directly in front of the aircraft**.

Ⓐ thump　**Ⓑ** douse　**Ⓒ** flout　**Ⓓ** nudge

中譯	這位飛行經驗豐富的駕駛員必須迅速將直升機略為偏右移動，以避免與飛行在直升機正前方的鳥相撞。 🅐 重擊　　　　　　🅑 浸入水中；熄滅（燈火） 🅒 公然藐視；嘲笑；嘲弄　🅓 （朝某方向）輕推
取樣	瀏覽全文，in order to所引導表「目的」的不定詞片語修飾前面的動詞片語 ＿＿＿＿＿ the helicopter to the right。解題關鍵在於修飾語，因此取樣修飾語中的表「目的」的不定詞片語to avoid
取樣	colliding with the bird flying directly in front of the aircraft（以避免與飛行在直升機正前方的鳥相撞）。
預測	空格內應填入和to avoid colliding with the bird flying directly in front of the aircraft語意緊密相關的動詞，從常理推斷，駕駛為了避免與飛行在直升機正前方的鳥相撞，所以將直升機略為偏右移動，預測選項 🅓 nudge（（朝某方向）輕推）符合這個語境。
檢驗	將 🅓 選項填入空格中檢驗句意。
確認	瀏覽上下句，整體句意連貫，確認答案為 🅓。本題的題型是modifier型，主要考表「目的」的不定詞片語修飾動詞片語。

5. Democracy continues **to be the strongest form of** ＿＿＿＿＿ **for Taiwan as the government looks to the challenges ahead.**

　🅐 prevention　　🅑 alliance　　🅒 maneuver　　🅓 defense

中譯	政府在面臨未來的挑戰時，民主制度仍然是台灣最堅固的防禦形式。 🅐 預防；預防方法　🅑 （國家、政黨等的）結盟、聯盟 🅒 操縱　　　　　　🅓 防禦
取樣	瀏覽全文，表「時間」的從屬連接詞as所引導的副詞子句修飾主要子句的動詞片語continues to be the strongest form of ＿＿＿＿＿ for Taiwan（仍然是台灣最堅固的形式）。解題關

取樣	鍵在於修飾語，因此取樣動詞片語looks to the challenges ahead（面臨未來的挑戰時）。此外，the strongest form of ＿＿＿＿＿ for Taiwan是主詞補語，以補足主詞意義上不足之處，因此關鍵詞應落在主詞補語上，但主詞補語挖空，應該從主詞找線索，因此取樣democracy（民主）。
預測	空格內應填入和looks to the challenges ahead和democracy語意緊密相關的名詞，從常理推斷，政府在面臨未來的挑戰時，民主制度可以讓人民團結一致，是最為堅固的防禦形式，預測選項 **D** defense（防禦）符合這個語境。
檢驗	將 **D** 選項填入空格中檢驗句意。
確認	瀏覽上下句，整體句意連貫，確認答案為 **D**。本題的題型是考修飾語：主詞補語、副詞子句修飾主要子句的動詞片語。

6. Today the famous photographer owns a fleet of drones in New York that he uses to shoot projects as ＿＿＿＿＿ **as BMW commercials, corporate events, and weddings.**

A lucrative　　**B** formidable　　**C** incidental　　**D** varied

中譯	現今這位著名的攝影師擁有紐約的一支無人機隊，他用來拍攝各種各樣的專案，如寶馬商業廣告、企業活動和婚禮。 **A** 可獲利的、賺錢的　　**B** 可怕的；令人畏懼的 **C** 附帶發生的；次要的　　**D** 各式各樣的；有變化的
取樣	瀏覽全文，as...as...結構中第一個as為指示副詞，第二個as為連接詞，表「如、像」的從屬連接詞as所引導的副詞片語修飾前面的as ＿＿＿＿＿（一樣 ＿＿＿＿＿）。解題關鍵在於修飾語，因此取樣名詞（片語）BMW commercials（寶馬商業廣告）、corporate events（企業活動）、weddings（婚禮）。而形容詞片語as ＿＿＿＿＿ 修飾前面的名詞projects（專案），但修飾語挖空，應該從被修飾語找線索，因此取樣projects（專案）。

168　Chapter 5　認識修飾語結構：MODIFIER 型

預測	空格內應填入和BMW commercials、corporate events、weddings和projects語意緊密相關的名詞，從常理推斷，作者提到寶馬商業廣告、企業活動和婚禮等各式各樣專案，預測選項 **D** varied（各式各樣的）符合這個語境。
檢驗	將 **D** 選項填入空格中檢驗句意。
確認	瀏覽上下句，整體句意連貫，確認答案為 **D**。本題的題型是考修飾語：形容詞片語修飾名詞、副詞片語修飾前面的形容詞片語。

7. One good way to _____ a complicated concept is **to provide visual aids such as charts, figures or concept maps.**

A exasperate　　**B** exacerbate　　**C** explicate　　**D** expatiate

中譯	闡明複雜概念的好方法是提供視覺輔助工具，如圖表、數字或概念圖。 **A** 刺激；激怒　　**B** 使惡化；使加劇 **C** 詳細解釋、闡明　　**D** 長篇大論；詳述
取樣	瀏覽全文，不定詞片語to provide visual aids such as charts, figures or concept maps（提供視覺輔助工具，如圖表、數字或概念圖）在be動詞之後擔任主詞補語補充說明主詞good way（好方法），主詞補語為句意焦點，因此取樣補語中的正面線索provide visual aids（提供視覺輔助工具）。此外，由to所引導的不定詞片語to _____ a complicated concept（_____ 複雜概念）修飾good way，也應具有正面含義，才能讓be動詞的前後的主詞和主詞補語皆保持正向的含義。
預測	空格內應填入和provide visual aids語意正向相關的動詞。依生活經驗推斷，提供視覺輔助工具的目的是為了闡明複雜概念，預測選項 **C** explicate（詳細解釋，闡明）符合這個語境。注意way的常用句型：One way to V is to V 是不定詞片語擔任主詞補語的常用句型。

檢驗	將 C 選項填入空格中檢驗句意。
確認	瀏覽上下句，整體句意連貫，確認答案為 C。本題的題型是考修飾語：主詞補語。所搭配的主詞補語都是句意焦點，本題句意的焦點在不定詞片語to provide visual aids such as charts, figures or concept maps。

8. The manager tried to _____ the angry customer **by offering a full refund for their defective product.**

   A mollify　**B** vilify　**C** stultify　**D** ramify　**E** petrify

中譯	經理對有瑕疵的產品藉由提供全額退款來安撫憤怒的顧客。 **A** 安撫、撫慰　　**B** 汙衊；誹謗 **C** 使顯得愚蠢、使（先前的努力等）無效 **D** 分叉、分枝　　**E** 使石化；使驚呆
取樣	瀏覽全文，表「藉由」的介系詞by所引導的副詞片語by offering a full refund for their defective product（藉由提供全額退款來彌補有瑕疵的產品）修飾主要子句的動詞。解題關鍵在於修飾語，因此取樣修飾語中的offering a full refund（提供全額退款）。
預測	空格內應填入和offering a full refund語意緊密相關的字詞，依常理推斷，大多是因為產品有瑕疵，經理為了安撫顧客，才提供全額退款，預測選項 **A** mollify（安撫、撫慰）符合這個語境。
檢驗	將 **A** 選項填入空格中檢驗句意。
確認	瀏覽上下句，整體句意連貫，確認答案為 **A**，正確答案就在題目上。本題的題型是考修飾語：介系詞by所引導的副詞片語修飾主要子句的動詞。

9. **To properly diagnose sickle cell disease in rural Kenya**, physicians at regional hospitals often strive to be _____ **when examining patients and performing predictive testing.**

Ⓐ impartial　　Ⓑ impecunious　　Ⓒ fatuous　　Ⓓ pernicious
Ⓔ puerile

中譯	為了能夠正確診斷肯亞農村地區的鐮刀型紅血球疾病，地區醫院的醫生在檢查病人和進行預測測試時，通常會盡力保持公正無私的。 Ⓐ 公平無私的；不偏不倚的　　Ⓑ 貧窮的；不名一文的 Ⓒ 愚蠢的；愚昧的　　Ⓓ 有害的、有毒的 Ⓓ 幼稚的；膚淺的
取樣	瀏覽全文，不定詞To所引導的表「目的」的不定詞片語修飾後面的動詞片語strive to be _____（盡力保持）。解題關鍵在於修飾語，因此取樣修飾語中的properly diagnose（正確診斷）。此外，表「時間」的從屬連接詞when所引導的副詞子句也是修飾前面的動詞片語strive to be _____（盡力保持），因此取樣examining patients（檢查病人）、performing predictive testing（進行預測性檢測）。
預測	空格內應填入和properly diagnose、examining patients、performing predictive testing語意緊密相關的字詞，依常理推斷，醫生在檢查病人和進行預測性檢測時，通常需要盡力保持公正無私。才能正確診斷出疾病，預測選項 Ⓐ impartial（公平的；不偏不倚的）符合這個語境。
檢驗	將 Ⓐ 選項填入空格中檢驗句意。
確認	瀏覽上下句，整體句意連貫，確認答案為 Ⓐ，正確答案就在題目上。本題的題型是考修飾語：表「目的」的不定詞片語修飾動詞片語、表「時間」的副詞子句也修飾前面的動詞片語。

10. The natural products industry is a(n) _____ market **that is projected to rapidly grow to $226 billion by 2018 with an annual growth rate of 8.6 percent.**

Ⓐ flagging　　Ⓑ burgeoning　　Ⓒ infuriating　　Ⓓ daunting

中譯	天然產品業是個快速發展的市場，預計到2018年將以8.6%的年增長率迅速增長至2,260億元。 Ⓐ 下垂的；萎靡的　　　　　Ⓑ 快速發展的 Ⓒ 使人極為生氣（或憤怒）的　Ⓓ 使人氣餒的
取樣	瀏覽全文，關係代名詞that引導限定形容詞子句that is projected to rapidly grow to $226 billion by 2018 with an annual growth rate of 8.6 percent（預計到2018年將以8.6%的年增長率迅速增長至2,260億元）修飾先行詞market。解題關鍵在於修飾語，因此取樣修飾語中的動詞（片語）is projected to rapidly grow。
預測	空格內應填入和is projected to rapidly grow語意緊密相關的字詞，從經濟學常識來判斷，天然產品業年增長率迅速增長至2,260億元，表示該行業是個快速發展的市場，預測選項 Ⓑ burgeoning（迅速發展的）符合這個語境。
檢驗	將 Ⓑ 選項填入空格中檢驗句意。
確認	瀏覽上下句，整體句意連貫，確認答案為 Ⓑ，正確答案就在題目上。本題的題型是考修飾語：形容詞子句修飾名詞。

11. Many so-to-speak politicians' interests are strictly _____, **which means they are interested only in the money or other personal advantages.**

Ⓐ meretricious　　Ⓑ meticulous　　Ⓒ mercenary　　Ⓓ mercurial

中譯	許多所謂的政客的利益完全是唯利是圖的，這意味著他們只對金錢或其他個人利益感興趣。 Ⓐ 華而不實的；虛有其表的　Ⓑ 細心的；小心翼翼的 Ⓒ 唯利是圖的、貪財的　　　Ⓓ 多變的；變幻莫測的

取樣	瀏覽全文，關係代名詞which引導非限定形容詞子句，which means they are interested only in the money or other personal advantages（這意味著他們只對金錢或其他個人利益感興趣）修飾前面mercenary (interests)，其中mercenary和interests語意是重複的，必須刪除，句意才會簡潔。解題關鍵在於修飾語，因此取樣修飾語中的動詞（片語）are interested only in the money or other personal advantages。
預測	空格內應填入和are interested only in the money or other personal advantages語意緊密相關的字詞，從常理來推斷，政客只對金錢或其他個人利益感興趣，表示他們唯利是圖，預測選項 **C** mercenary（唯利是圖的、貪財的）符合這個語境。
檢驗	將 **C** 選項填入空格中檢驗句意。
確認	瀏覽上下句，整體句意連貫，確認答案為 **C**，正確答案就在題目上。本題的題型是考修飾語：形容詞子句修飾名詞interests，因語意重複而省略。

12. **After seeing his favorite toy taken away by his brother**, the little boy wailed ＿＿＿＿ in the living room and nothing seemed able to stop him.

   A viciously　　**B** hysterically　　**C** abruptly　　**D** feebly

中譯	在看到最喜歡的玩具被哥哥拿走後，小男孩在客廳裡歇斯底里地放聲大哭，似乎什麼都無法阻止他（哭泣）。 **A** 邪惡地；惡意地　　**B** 歇斯底里地 **C** 意外地、突然地　　**D** 衰弱地；無力地
取樣	瀏覽全文，表「時間」的從屬連接詞After所引導的省略型副詞子句修飾後方主要子句動詞wailed（大哭）。解題關鍵在於修飾語，因此取樣修飾語中的seeing his favorite toy taken away by his brother（看到最喜歡的玩具被哥哥拿走）。還原完整的副詞子句如下：After the little boy saw his favorite toy taken away by his brother。此外，藉標示詞and猜測前後語意呈現負面

考古題測驗與解析　173

取樣	並列關係，意義必須前因後果一致，取樣後面的 nothing seemed able to stop him（似乎什麼都無法阻止他）。
預測	空格內應填入和（因）seeing his favorite toy taken away by his brother、（果）nothing seemed able to stop him (from crying)因果語意相關的字詞，從生活經驗推斷，小男孩在看到最喜歡的玩具被哥哥拿走，哭得歇斯底里，似乎沒有麼可以阻止他，預測選項 Ⓑ hysterically（歇斯底里地）符合這個語境。
檢驗	將 Ⓑ 選項填入空格中檢驗句意。
確認	瀏覽上下句，整體句意連貫，確認答案為 Ⓑ。本題的題型是考修飾語：表「時間」先後的副詞子句修飾主要子句的動詞（wailed），因先拿走，後哭泣。

13. The Zoo has been looking after young chimps, _____ by customs officials when poachers smuggled them over the border.

Ⓐ vindicated　　Ⓑ confiscated　　Ⓒ delegated　　Ⓓ penetrated

中譯	動物園一直在照顧一群年幼的黑猩猩，這些黑猩猩是偷獵者偷運過境時被海關官員沒收的。 Ⓐ 證明……正確；證明……是真的 Ⓑ （尤指作為懲罰）沒收、把……充公 Ⓒ 授（權）；把（工作、權力等）委託（給下級） Ⓓ 貫穿；滲透
取樣	瀏覽全文，過去分詞片語用來修飾主要子句內受詞 young chimps，是非限定形容詞子句, which were _____ by customs officials省略而來的，但修飾語挖空，應從被修飾語找線索，因此取樣 chimps（黑猩猩）。此外，表「時間」的從屬連接詞 when 所引導的副詞子句修飾前方的空格（被動動詞）_____。解題關鍵在於修飾語，因此取樣修飾語中的動詞 smuggled them（走私黑猩猩）。注意，此處的 them 指的就是先行詞 chimps。

預測	空格內應填入和chimps、smuggled them負面語意相關的過去分詞，從常理來推論，海關關員發現違法走私的黑猩猩會沒收充公，預測選項 **B** confiscated（（尤指作為懲罰）沒收）符合這個語境。
檢驗	將 **B** 選項填入空格中檢驗句意。
確認	瀏覽上下句，整體句意連貫，確認答案為 **B**。題型是考修飾語：過去分詞片語用來修飾主要子句內的名詞、表「時間」的副詞子句修飾前面的被動動詞（confiscated）。

14. The host of the Golden Horse Film ceremony handled the unexpected incident **with great** _____.
    A aplomb **B** autonomy **C** jeopardy **D** testimony

中譯	金馬影展典禮主持人非常冷靜沉著處理突發事件。 **A** 鎮定；沉著；泰然自若　**B** 自治；自治權 **C** 危險　　　　　　　　　**D** 證據；證詞
取樣	瀏覽全文，介系詞with+抽象名詞引導狀態副詞片語（如with care=carefully）with great _____（非 _____）修飾動詞handled（處理）。解題關鍵在於修飾語，但修飾語中有空格，因此取樣被修飾語中的動詞handled。
預測	空格內應填入和handled語意緊密相關的字詞，一般來說，典禮主持人處理突發事件時不外乎是荒腔走板、不知所措、中規中矩、臨危不亂等各種狀況，檢視四個選項，只有選項 **A** aplomb（鎮定；沉著；泰然自若）符合這個語境。
檢驗	將 **A** 選項填入空格中檢驗句意。
確認	瀏覽上下句，整體句意連貫，確認答案為 **A**。本題的題型是考修飾語：介系詞with引導引導狀態副詞片語修飾動詞。

15. A recent major research found the vigor of a person's hand-grip could predict the risk of heart attacks and strokes, and was **a stronger predictor of death than checking _____ blood pressure.**

Ⓐ synchronous　　Ⓑ systolic　　Ⓒ synergistic　　Ⓓ systematic

中譯	近期一項重大研究發現，一個人手的握力強度可以預測心臟病和中風的風險，是一個比起測量心臟收縮壓更能預測死亡風險的指標。 Ⓐ 同時發生（或存在）的；同步的　　Ⓑ 心臟收縮的 Ⓒ （藥物等）配合作用的、協同作用的 Ⓓ 成體系的；系統的
取樣	瀏覽全文，a stronger predictor of death than checking _____ blood pressure（比起測量 _____ 壓更能預測死亡風險）在be動詞之後擔任主詞補語補充說明主詞the vigor of a person's hand-grip（一個人手的握力強度），主詞補語為句意焦點，因此優先取樣a stronger predictor of death（一個更能預測死亡風險的指標），但因主詞補語有空格，因此取樣主詞the vigor of a person's hand-grip（一個人手的握力強度）。此外，藉標示詞and猜測前後語意呈現正面並列關係，意義必須前因後果一致，取樣前面的動詞片語predict the risk of heart attacks and strokes（預測心臟病和中風的風險）。
預測	空格內應填入和the vigor of a person's hand-grip、a stronger predictor of death、predict the risk of heart attacks and strokes語意緊密相關的字詞，根據醫學常識，收縮壓上升會增死亡風險，藉由測量收縮壓可以預測死亡風險，但根據題意，個人手的握力強度比測量收縮壓更能夠預測死亡風險，只有選項 Ⓑ systolic（心臟收縮的）符合這個語境。
檢驗	將 Ⓑ 選項填入空格中檢驗句意。
確認	瀏覽上下句，整體句意連貫，確認答案為 Ⓑ。本題的題型是考修飾語：主詞補語。

16. She is an _____ movie star **who thinks she's some sort of goddess and likes to tell other people what to do.**

Ⓐ impassive　　Ⓑ immutable　　Ⓒ ingenuous　　Ⓓ imperious

中譯	她是一位傲慢的電影明星，真以為自己是個女神，喜歡告訴別人該做什麼。 Ⓐ 冷靜的；不動感情的　　Ⓑ 不可改變的；永恆不變的 Ⓒ 無心機的；天真無邪的　　Ⓓ 傲慢的、專橫的
取樣	瀏覽全文，關係代名詞who引導限定形容詞子句who thinks she's some sort of goddess and likes to tell other people what to do（以為自己是個女神，喜歡告訴別人該做什麼）修飾前面的名詞movie star（電影明星）。解題關鍵在於修飾語，因此取樣修飾語中的動詞（片語）thinks she's some sort of goddess和tell other people what to do。
預測	空格內應填入和thinks she's some sort of goddess、tell other people what to do語意緊密相關的字詞，從常理來推斷，一個自以為是個女神，喜歡命令別人做事的人必定是個傲慢的人，選預測項 Ⓓ imperious（傲慢的、專橫的）符合這個語境。
檢驗	將 Ⓓ 選項填入空格中檢驗句意。
確認	瀏覽上下句，整體句意連貫，確認答案為 Ⓓ，正確答案就在題目上。本題的題型是考修飾語：形容詞子句修飾名詞。

17. This fledgling boxer is now ready to test his _____ **by signing up for a nationwide boxing match.**

Ⓐ mettle　　Ⓑ coffer　　Ⓒ coiffure　　Ⓓ lineup

中譯	這位初出茅廬的拳擊手現在準備藉由報名參加全國拳擊賽來測試自己的勇氣。 Ⓐ 氣質；勇氣；毅力 Ⓑ （舊時的）保險櫃、金庫　　Ⓒ 髮式；髮型 Ⓓ 人的行列；（為某種目的而聚集的）成員、結構

取樣	瀏覽全文，表示「藉由」的介系詞by所引導的副詞片語修飾前面的動詞片語test his ＿＿＿＿＿＿（考驗他的 ＿＿＿＿＿＿）。解題關鍵在於修飾語，因此取樣修飾語中的動名詞片語signing up for a nationwide boxing match（報名參加全國拳擊賽）。
預測	空格內應填入和signing up for a nationwide boxing match語意緊密相關的名詞，從常理來推斷，初出茅廬的拳擊手報名參加全國拳擊賽是為了測試自己的勇氣，預測選項 Ⓐ mettle（勇氣）符合這個語境。
檢驗	將 Ⓐ 選項填入空格中檢驗句意。
確認	瀏覽上下句，整體句意連貫，確認答案為 Ⓐ。本題的題型是考修飾語：by所引導的副詞片語修飾動詞

18. The ＿＿＿＿＿＿ of a particular place or group of people are **the customs and behaviors that are typically found in that place or group**.

Ⓐ morals　　Ⓑ mores　　Ⓒ mussels　　Ⓓ molds

中譯	特定地方或群體的風俗習慣是指在該地方或群體中通常存在的習俗和行為。 Ⓐ 品行、道德　　Ⓑ（一集團、社會的）習慣；習俗（尤指一般社會所能接受的標準與道德界線） Ⓒ 蚌；貽貝　　Ⓓ 模具；黴菌
取樣	瀏覽全文，名詞片語the customs and behaviors（習俗和行為）在be動詞之後擔任主詞補語補充說明主詞The ＿＿＿＿＿＿，主詞補語為句意焦點，因此優先取樣名詞片語the customs and behaviors（習俗和行為）。
預測	空格內應填入和the customs and behaviors語意緊密相關的名詞，預測選項 Ⓑ mores（風俗習慣）符合這個語境。
檢驗	將 Ⓑ 選項填入空格中檢驗句意。
確認	瀏覽上下句，整體句意連貫，確認答案為 Ⓑ。本題的題型是考修飾語：主詞補語。

19. A _____ , **a vote in which everyone (or nearly everyone) of voting age can take part**, was held on Thursday, June 23rd, 2016, to decide whether the UK should leave or remain in the European Union.

Ⓐ transition　　Ⓑ referendum　　Ⓒ forfeiture　　Ⓓ penalty

中譯	2016年6月23日星期四，舉行了一場<u>全民公投</u>，達到投票年齡的每個人都可以參與，以決定英國是否應該脫歐或留歐。 Ⓐ 過渡；轉變　　Ⓑ 全民投票 Ⓒ 喪失；沒收　　Ⓓ 懲罰；處罰
取樣	瀏覽全文，同位語a vote in which everyone (or nearly everyone) of voting age can take part是補充說明前面的空格中的名詞，解題關鍵在於同位語。
預測	空格內應填入和in which everyone (or nearly everyone) of voting age can take part語意緊密相關的字詞，預測選項 Ⓑ referendum（全民公投）符合這個語境。
檢驗	將 Ⓑ 選項填入空格中檢驗句意。
確認	瀏覽上下句，整體句意連貫，確認答案為 Ⓑ，正確答案就在題目上。本題的題型是考：同位語。請參閱160頁同位語的線索。

20. The material, color and design of our watch products can be modified or tailor-made for customers **upon** _____ .

Ⓐ request　　Ⓑ resilience　　Ⓒ oblivion　　Ⓓ oblation

中譯	我們手錶產品的材料、顏色和設計可以根據客戶的<u>請求</u>來修改或量身訂做。 Ⓐ 要求、請求　　　　　Ⓑ 彈力；適應力 Ⓒ 遺忘（的狀態）；忘卻　Ⓓ （對神的）奉獻；供品
取樣	瀏覽全文，表「根據」的介系詞upon所引導的副詞片語修飾主要子句的被動動詞be modified or tailor-made（來修改或量身訂做）。解題關鍵在於修飾語，但修飾語挖空，因此取樣被修飾語中的modified（修改）和複合形容詞tailor-made（訂製）。

預測	空格內應填入和modified、tailor-made語意緊密相關的字詞，依常理推斷，手錶產品的材料、顏色和設計要做修改或量身訂做，那必定是為了符合客戶的要求，預測選項 Ⓐ request（要求、請求）符合這個語境。注意：upon request意思是「一經請求、根據要求」。
檢驗	將 Ⓐ 選項填入空格中檢驗句意。
確認	瀏覽上下句，整體句意連貫，確認答案為 Ⓐ，正確答案就在題目上。本題的題型是考修飾語：介系詞upon所引導的副詞片語修飾主要子句的被動動詞。

21. The speaker's attempts to divert attention from the real issue **by bringing up** _____ **points** only served to confuse the audience.

Ⓐ unanimous　　Ⓑ tangential　　Ⓒ charismatic　　Ⓓ incorrigible

中譯	演講者藉由提出離題的論點，試圖將注意力從真正的問題上轉移，但卻只讓聽眾感到困惑。 Ⓐ （決定或意見）一致的、一致同意的 Ⓑ 離題的；不相干的 Ⓒ 有超凡魅力的；有號召力（或感召力）的 Ⓓ 無法改正的；無藥可救的
取樣	瀏覽全文，表「藉由」的介系詞by所引導的副詞片語修飾前面的動詞片語divert attention from the real issue（將注意力從真正的問題上轉移）。解題關鍵在於修飾語，但修飾語挖空，因此取樣被修飾語中的divert attention from the real issue。
預測	空格內應填入和divert attention from the real issue語意緊密相關的字詞，依常理推斷，講者要從真正的問題轉移聽眾的注意力，常見的作法是提出離題的論點來混淆視聽，預測選項 Ⓑ tangential（離題的；不相干的）符合這個語境。
檢驗	將 Ⓑ 選項填入空格中檢驗句意。

| 確認 | 瀏覽上下句，整體句意連貫，確認答案為 **B**。本題考的重點是「憑什麼動作來修飾動詞」如：how to divert attention from the real issue? 最簡潔的方式用介系詞片語by (by means of的省略)+Ving，「藉什麼動作來修飾動詞」。 |

22. The _____ atmosphere of the old abandoned mansion was enough to send shivers down anyone's spine, **making it clear that the rumors of ghosts haunting the place were not entirely unfounded.**

   Ⓐ prescient　　Ⓑ sinister　　Ⓒ ostensible　　Ⓓ irascible

中譯	這座古老廢棄的大宅子散發出的不祥氣氛足以讓任何人毛骨悚然，顯然關於鬼魂在此出沒的傳聞並非完全沒有根據。 Ⓐ 預知的；有先見之明的　　Ⓑ 不祥的、凶兆的；邪惡的 Ⓒ 表面的；假裝的　　　　　Ⓓ 易怒的；暴躁的
取樣	瀏覽全文，現在分詞片語, making it clear that the rumors of ghosts haunting the place were not entirely unfounded是由非限定形容詞子句, which makes it clear that the rumors of ghosts haunting the place were not entirely unfounded省略而來的，修飾前面整個句子。解題關鍵在於修飾語，因此取樣修飾語中的名詞片語the rumors of ghosts haunting the place（鬼魂在此出沒的傳聞）。
預測	空格內應填入和the rumors of ghosts haunting the place語意緊密相關的形容詞，修飾名詞atmosphere。從生活經驗推斷，凡是有鬧鬼傳聞的房子，都會給人一種陰森、險惡的、不祥的氛圍，預測選項 Ⓑ sinister（不祥的、凶兆的）符合這個語境。
檢驗	將 Ⓑ 選項填入空格中檢驗句意。
確認	瀏覽上下句，整體句意連貫，確認答案為 Ⓑ。本題的題型是考修飾語：現在分詞片語修飾前面的整個句子。

23. Whatever consensus scholars may have reached has been achieved on the basis of _____ assumptions **made without fully and conscientiously analyzing currently available data.**

Ⓐ tenuous　Ⓑ sturdy　Ⓒ informative　Ⓓ cognizant

中譯	無論學者可能達成什麼樣的共識，都是源自於站不住腳的假設，而這些假設並沒有充分且認真地分析目前可用的數據。 Ⓐ（根據等）站不住腳的；（區別等）微小的 Ⓑ 結實的；堅固的　Ⓒ 提供有用訊息的；給予知識的 Ⓓ 認識的；意識到的
取樣	瀏覽全文，過去分詞片語made without fully and conscientiously analyzing currently available data是由限定形容詞子句which were made without fully and conscientiously analyzing currently available data省略而來的，修飾前面的名詞assumptions（假設）。解題關鍵在於修飾語，因此取樣修飾語中的由否定詞without所引導的介系詞片語without fully and conscientiously analyzing currently available data（並未充分且認真地分析目前可用的數據）。
預測	空格內應填入和without fully and conscientiously analyzing currently available data語意緊密相關的形容詞，修飾並說明名詞assumptions。從常理推斷，在未充分且認真地分析目前可用的數據情況下所做的假設，大多是站不住腳的，預測選項 Ⓐ tenuous（站不住腳的）符合這個語境。
檢驗	將 Ⓐ 選項填入空格中檢驗句意。
確認	瀏覽上下句，整體句意連貫，確認答案為 Ⓐ。本題的題型是考修飾語：過去分詞片語修飾前面的名詞。

24. The industry is being _____ **by high interest rates and inflation**; investors and economists are seriously worried about the current situation.

Ⓐ dispensed　Ⓑ prevailed　Ⓒ glittered　Ⓓ crippled

中譯	產業在高利率和高通膨中嚴重受損；投資者和經濟學家對目前的狀況深感擔心。 Ⓐ 分配、分發　　Ⓑ 盛行；普及 Ⓒ 閃亮；閃耀　　Ⓓ 嚴重損壞；嚴重削弱
取樣	瀏覽全文，介系詞by所引導的副詞片語by high interest rates and inflation修飾主要子句的被動動詞is being _____（正被……）。解題關鍵在於修飾語，因此取樣修飾語中的名詞（片語）high interest rates（高利率）和inflation（通貨膨脹）。此外，藉分號（;）猜測前後句語意呈現負面並列，分號代替對等連接詞，連接兩個負面緊密的子句，取樣後句的seriously worried（深感擔心）。
預測	空格內應填入和high interest rates、inflation、seriously worried語意緊密相關具有「負面」含義的被動動詞，根據經濟學基本常識判斷，高利率和通貨膨脹會嚴重衝擊產業的發展，情況令人憂心，預測選項 Ⓓ crippled（嚴重損壞；嚴重削弱）符合這個語境。
檢驗	將 Ⓓ 選項填入空格中檢驗句意。
確認	瀏覽上下句，整體句意連貫，確認答案為 Ⓓ。本題的題型是modifier：介系詞by所引導的副詞片語修飾主要子句的被動動詞。

25. Recent TV shows about Cold War spies feature _____ men and women **who look like your neighbors and lead seemingly normal lives.**

Ⓐ nondescript　　Ⓑ aggregated　　Ⓒ classified　　Ⓓ synonymous

中譯	最近關於冷戰間諜的電視劇，演員都是相貌平庸無奇看似過一般生活的市井小民。 Ⓐ （人或事物）沒有明顯特徵的；平庸無奇的　Ⓑ 聚集的 Ⓒ （資訊）機密的；分類的　　　　　　　　Ⓓ 同義的

取樣	瀏覽全文，關係代名詞who引導限定形容詞子句who look like your neighbors and lead seemingly normal lives（相貌平庸無奇看似過一般生活的）修飾前面的名詞men and women（男女，市井小民）。解題關鍵在於修飾語，因此取樣修飾語中的動詞（片語）look like your neighbors和lead seemingly normal lives。
預測	空格內應填入和look like your neighbors、lead seemingly normal lives語意緊密相關的形容詞，從上下文來推斷，電影中描述的冷戰間諜是看起來與鄰居無異、過著看似正常生活的平凡男女，預測選項 Ⓐ nondescript（平庸無奇的）符合這個語境。注意，feature當動詞用，意思是「由……主演、擔任主角」。
檢驗	將 Ⓐ 選項填入空格中檢驗句意。
確認	瀏覽上下句，整體句意連貫，確認答案為 Ⓐ，正確答案就在題目上。本題的題型是考修飾語：形容詞子句修飾名詞。

26. The once mild-mannered accountant went _____ when he discovered that his co-worker had been promoted over him, **smashing his computer and throwing papers all around the office in a fit of rage.**

   Ⓐ berserk   Ⓑ austere   Ⓒ amicable   Ⓓ forlorn

中譯	在發現同事竟然比他升遷到更高的職位時，原本溫文儒雅的會計師，突然<u>發狂</u>，在憤怒之下他砸碎了電腦，還在辦公室到處亂扔文件。 Ⓐ 狂暴的；暴跳如雷的　　Ⓑ（生活等）禁慾的；質樸的 Ⓒ 友好的；和睦的　　　　Ⓓ 孤苦伶仃的；孤獨淒涼的
取樣	瀏覽全文，現在分詞片語, smashing his computer and throwing papers all around the office in a fit of rage（砸碎了電腦，憤怒之下還在辦公室四處亂扔文件）是從and smashed his computer and threw papers all around the office in a fit of rage改變而成，至於如何改，請參閱150頁B(5)。解題關鍵在於修飾語，因此取

取樣	樣修飾語中的現在分詞smashing his computer（砸碎了電腦）、throwing papers all around the office（在辦公室四處亂扔文件）和介系詞片語in a fit of rage（憤怒之下）。
預測	空格內應填入和smashing his computer、throwing papers all around the office、尤其是in a fit of rage負面語意相關的字詞，依常理推斷，溫文儒雅的會計師在得知同事升遷到比他高的職位，摔壞電腦，盛怒下又亂丟文件，預測選項 Ⓐ berserk（狂暴的；暴跳如雷的）符合這個語境。注意：go意思是「變成……的狀態」，其後補語多為形容詞，是全句句意的焦點，如go mad（發瘋）、go berserk（發狂）、go blind（變瞎）、go bad（變壞）。
檢驗	將 Ⓐ 選項填入空格中檢驗句意。
確認	瀏覽上下句，整體句意連貫，確認答案為 Ⓐ。本題的題型是考現在分詞取代連接詞and。改變前的句子： The once mild-mannered accountant went (V1) berserk when he discovered that his co-worker had been promoted over him, and smashed (V2) his computer and threw (V3) papers all around the office in a fit of rage. 改變後的句子： The once mild-mannered accountant went berserk when he discovered that his co-worker had been promoted over him, smashing his computer and throwing papers all around the office in a fit of rage.（請參閱150頁B(5)的說明例。）

27. The New Jersey hospital's emergency department is one of a few in the nation with a _____ care program, a growing specialty that gives patients more control over their treatment and life in their final months or days.

   Ⓐ palliative   Ⓑ dismissive   Ⓒ meager   Ⓓ frilly

中譯	紐澤西州醫院的急診部是全國少數擁有安寧療護方案的醫院之一，這是一個不斷發展的醫學專科，讓患者在生命最後的幾個月或幾天擁有更多對治療和生活的掌控權。 Ⓐ 減輕的；（暫時）緩和的　Ⓑ 輕蔑的；鄙視的 Ⓒ 不足的、缺乏的　　　　　Ⓓ 鑲飾邊的；多褶邊的
取樣	瀏覽全文，同位語 a growing specialty that gives patients more control over their treatment and life in their final months or days（這是一個不斷發展的醫學專科，讓患者在生命最後的幾個月或幾天擁有更多對治療和生活的掌控權）是補充說明前面的名詞片語 a _____ care program。解題關鍵在於修飾語，因此取樣動詞片語 gives patients more control over their treatment and life。
預測	空格內應填入和 gives patients more control over their treatment and life 語意緊密相關的字詞，根據醫學知識，安寧療護方案是一種致力於提供對患者生命最後階段的綜合性治療和支持的醫療專案。這種治療方法的目標是尊重患者的價值觀和意願來減輕患者的痛苦和不適，並提高其生活品質，預測選項 Ⓐ palliative（減輕的；（暫時）緩和的）符合這個語境。
檢驗	將 Ⓐ 選項填入空格中檢驗句意。
確認	瀏覽上下句，整體句意連貫，確認答案為 Ⓐ，正確答案就在題目上。本題的題型是考：同位語。

28. The escalating _____ of the dictator towards his neighbors was **met with growing concern and condemnation from the international community.**

Ⓐ schadenfreude　Ⓑ harbinger　Ⓒ belligerence　Ⓓ pluviosity

中譯	獨裁者對鄰國不斷升高的敵意，受到國際社會越來越多的關注和譴責。 Ⓐ 幸災樂禍　　　Ⓑ （常指壞的）預兆、兆頭 Ⓒ 敵意、好戰性　Ⓓ 多雨性

文法解說	原句：S + V (meet) + O + adv ph： 〔主詞不必或無法言明〕met the escalating belligerence of the dictator towards his neighbors with growing concern and condemnation from the international community. 將受詞作為談話的主題（topic）改為被動： S + be met + adv ph： The escalating belligerence of the dictator towards his neighbors was met with growing concern and condemnation from the international community.
取樣	瀏覽全文，帶有負面含義的介系詞片語（副詞片語）with growing concern and condemnation from the international community（遭受國際社會越來越多的關注和譴責）修飾動詞 met，因此及物動詞 meet 的受詞也要有負面的含義。解題關鍵在於修飾語，因此優先取樣名詞片語 growing concern（越來越多的關注）和 condemnation（譴責）。
預測	空格內應填入和 growing concern、condemnation 語意緊密相關的名詞，按常理推斷，獨裁者會受到國際社會越來越多的關注和譴責，無疑是其對鄰國產生敵意，或有侵略性，預測選項 ❸ belligerence（敵意、好戰）符合這個語境。
檢驗	將 ❸ 選項填入空格中檢驗句意。
確認	瀏覽上下句，整體句意連貫，確認答案為 ❸。本題的題型是考修飾語：介系詞片語（副詞片語）修飾動詞。

29. This month Taiwanese nationals and eligible foreign residents can receive NT$6,000 tax _____ **from the surplus tax revenue of last year.**

Ⓐ attrition　　Ⓑ attribute　　Ⓒ rebate　　Ⓓ evasion

中譯	這個月每一位台灣國民和符合資格的外國居民都可以從去年的稅款盈餘中領取新台幣6,000元的退還稅款。 Ⓐ（尤指給敵人造成的）削弱、消耗 Ⓑ 歸屬；屬性　　Ⓒ 退稅款　　Ⓓ 躲避；規避

取樣	瀏覽全文，介系詞from所引導的副詞片語from the surplus tax revenue of last year（從去年的稅款盈餘）修飾前面的動詞片語receive NT$6,000 tax _____（領取新台幣6,000元的退還稅款）。解題關鍵在於修飾語，因此取樣修飾語中的the surplus tax revenue（稅款盈餘）。
預測	空格內應填入和the surplus tax revenue語意緊密相關的字詞，依常理推斷，政府有稅款盈餘，就會有機會還稅於民，預測選項 ❻ (tax) rebate（退還稅款）符合這個語境。
檢驗	將 ❻ 選項填入空格中檢驗句意。
確認	瀏覽上下句，整體句意連貫，確認答案為 ❻。本題考的重點是：副詞（片語）修飾動詞（片語）。參閱第18頁祕訣8。

30. According to Norse mythology, the mischievous god Loki, **a shape-shifting deity known for his _____**, would often transform into animals in order to interfere with the other gods' plans and alliances.

  Ⓐ avarice　　Ⓑ chicanery　　Ⓒ apathy　　Ⓓ diffidence

中譯	根據北歐神話，惡作劇之神洛基是變形之神，以詭計聞名，他經常變成各種動物來干擾其他眾神的計劃和聯盟。 Ⓐ 貪財、貪心　　Ⓑ 詭計；詭辯 Ⓒ 冷漠；淡漠　　Ⓓ 缺乏自信；膽怯
取樣	瀏覽全文，同位語a shape-shifting deity known for his _____，（變形之神，以 _____ 聞名）是補充說明前面的名詞the mischievous god Loki（惡作劇之神洛基）。遇有形容詞後接名詞的結構，解題關鍵在於修飾語，因此取樣形容詞mischievous。參閱第15頁祕訣5。
預測	空格內應填入和mischievous語意緊密相關的字詞，根據基本常識來推斷，惡作劇之神洛基應該是以他的詭計聞名，預測選項 Ⓑ chicanery（詭計；詭辯）符合這個語境。注意表「有名」的原因，介系詞用for，是語意的焦點。

| 檢驗 | 將 Ⓑ 選項填入空格中檢驗句意。 |
| 確認 | 瀏覽上下句，整體句意連貫，確認答案為 Ⓑ，正確答案就在題目上。本題的題型是考：同位語。 |

31. As long as monkeypox spreads faster than health authorities can contain it, there is a risk **that it is going to _____ new variants, potentially driving up the death toll.**

Ⓐ spawn　　Ⓑ scaffold　　Ⓒ assess　　Ⓓ stalk　　Ⓔ array

中譯	只要猴痘的傳播速度快於衛生當局的遏制速度，就存在產生新變種病毒的風險，可能增加死亡人數。 Ⓐ 大量地產生；引起　Ⓑ 給（建築物）架設鷹架 Ⓒ 評估（價值、重要性等）；估算（稅額、罰款等）的數額 Ⓓ 偷偷接近、潛近（獵物或人） Ⓔ 盛裝；排列（軍隊）
取樣	瀏覽全文，現在分詞片語, potentially driving up the death toll（可能會增加死亡人數）是從which will potentially drive up the death toll改變而成。現在分詞片語修飾前面的名詞new variants（新變種病毒）。解題關鍵在於修飾語，因此取樣修飾語中的現在分詞片語driving up the death toll（導致死亡人數上升）。
預測	空格內應填入driving up the death toll負面的語意相關的字詞，依常理推斷，猴痘傳播速度太快，易產生變種病毒，造成死亡人數的上升，預測選項 Ⓐ spawn（大量地產生）符合這個語境。
檢驗	將 Ⓐ 選項填入空格中檢驗句意。
確認	瀏覽上下句，整體句意連貫，確認答案為 Ⓐ。本題的題型是考現在分詞片語修飾前面的名詞。

32. Guatemala is the country with the second-greatest income _____ **between rich and poor in Latin America**, behind only Brazil, according to the World Bank.

Ⓐ disparity　　**Ⓑ** oblivion　　**Ⓒ** moratorium　　**Ⓓ** contraception

中譯	根據世界銀行資料，在拉丁美洲各國中，瓜地馬拉的貧富差距位居第二，僅次於巴西。 Ⓐ 不相稱、不均衡、不等　　Ⓑ 被遺忘；被忘卻 Ⓒ （武器之製造或債務之償還）延期償付 Ⓓ 避孕（法）；節育（法）
取樣	瀏覽全文，表「在……之間」的介系詞between所引導的形容詞片語between rich and poor in Latin America（在拉丁美洲各國中貧和富之間的）修飾前面的空格。解題關鍵在於修飾語，因此取樣修飾語中的形容詞片語between rich and poor in Latin America。
預測	空格內應填入和between rich and poor in Latin America負面語意相關的字詞，依常理推斷，貧和富之間的差距很大，預測選項 Ⓐ disparity（不相稱、不均衡、不等）符合這個語境。
檢驗	將 Ⓐ 選項填入空格中檢驗句意。
確認	瀏覽上下句，整體句意連貫，確認答案為 Ⓐ。本題的題型是考形容詞片語修飾名詞。

33. The best way **to avoid committing** _____ is **to always document the sources you use and respect the intellectual property rights of others.**

Ⓐ suicide　　**Ⓑ** vandalism　　**Ⓒ** harassment　　**Ⓓ** plagiarism

中譯	避免抄襲最好的方法是永遠記錄你所使用資料的來源，並尊重他人的智慧財產權。 Ⓐ 自殺　　Ⓑ （對公物的）惡意破壞；恣意毀壞他人財產罪 Ⓒ 煩惱；侵擾　　Ⓓ 抄襲；剽竊

取樣	瀏覽全文，不定詞片語to always document the sources you use and respect the intellectual property rights of others（永遠記錄你所使用資料的來源，並尊重他人的智慧財產權）在be動詞之後用不定詞片語擔任主詞補語，補充說明主詞The best way（最好的方法），主詞補語為句意焦點，因此優先取樣不定詞片語to document the sources（記錄資料的來源）、respect the intellectual property rights of others（尊重他人的智慧財產權）。此外，不定詞片語to avoid committing ＿＿＿＿＿＿（避免 ＿＿＿＿＿＿）是用來修飾The best way，和主詞補語一樣都是用來修飾主詞，因此應該和主詞補語的意思相近。
預測	因為空格前有to avoid 'try not to go near someone or something'（躲避，避閃）的語意屬性是負面的（negative），因此空格內應填入和document the sources、respect the intellectual property rights of others語意相反的名詞，預測選項 **D** plagiarism（抄襲；剽竊）符合這個語境。參閱124頁第4題的avoid用法。
檢驗	將 **D** 選項填入空格中檢驗句意。
確認	瀏覽上下句，整體句意連貫，確認答案為 **D**。本題的題型是考修飾語：主詞補語、不定詞片語修飾名詞。本題常用的不定詞片語句型：The best way to V is to V。

34. This world-renowned restaurant, **one of the most luxurious in the city**, charges ＿＿＿＿＿＿ prices **only the rich and famous can afford.**

Ⓐ ingrained　　**Ⓑ** redundant　　**Ⓒ** consecutive　　**Ⓓ** exorbitant

中譯	這家享譽世界的餐廳，是本市最奢華的餐廳之一，收取的價格高得離譜，只有富人和名人才消費得起。 **Ⓐ** 根深蒂固的　　**Ⓑ** 多餘的；不需要的 **Ⓒ** 連續不斷的　　**Ⓓ** 過高的（索價或要求）；高得離譜的
取樣	瀏覽全文，同位語one of the most luxurious (restaurant) in the city（本市中最奢華的餐廳之一）是補充說明前面的名詞This world-renowned restaurant（這家享譽世界的餐廳）。解題關鍵

考古題測驗與解析　191

取樣	在於修飾語，因此取樣修飾語中的形容詞most luxurious（最奢華的）。此外，形容詞子句(which) only the rich and famous can afford（只有富人和名人才消費得起）修飾前面的名詞prices（價格），因此取樣only the rich and famous can afford。請參閱第16頁祕訣7。
預測	空格內應填入和most luxurious、only the rich and famous can afford語意緊密相關的字詞，根據常識來推斷，最奢華的餐廳之一收費必定昂貴，只有富人和名人消費得起，預測選項 **D** exorbitant（過高的；高得離譜的）符合這個語境。
檢驗	將 **D** 選項填入空格中檢驗句意。
確認	瀏覽上下句，整體句意連貫，確認答案為 **D**，正確答案就在題目上。本題的題型是考：同位語。

35. When Pamela moved with her husband from Germany to the United States, she didn't feel like _____ there **until they had their first son a few years later.**

Ⓐ putting down roots　　**Ⓑ** bringing to heel
Ⓒ calling the tune　　　**Ⓓ** cracking the whip

中譯	帕梅拉和丈夫從德國搬到美國幾年後，迎來了第一個兒子，她才想要在當地<u>落地生根</u>。 **Ⓐ** 在新的土地上向下紮根；落地生根 **Ⓑ** 使某人緊跟在後；使某人就範；迫使某人服從（紀律） **Ⓒ** 發施令　　**Ⓓ** 威逼、施威（使某人表現更好或更賣力）
取樣	瀏覽全文，表示「直到……才」的從屬連接詞not...until所引導的副詞子句until they had their first son a few years later（直到幾年後迎來第一個兒子）修飾前面的動詞片語not feel like _____ there（才想要在當地），因此取樣had their first son。注意：until用於否定句，其意是「在……以前」（before）。

192　Chapter 5　認識修飾語結構：MODIFIER 型

預測	空格內應填入和had their first son語意緊密相關的字詞，根據生活經驗來推斷，移民者在沒孩子之前，並不想在新的土地上向下紮根，但移民者有了孩子後很容易產生在當地落地生根的想法，預測選項 Ⓐ putting down roots（落地生根）符合這個語境。
檢驗	將 Ⓐ 選項填入空格中檢驗句意。
確認	瀏覽上下句，整體句意連貫，確認答案為 Ⓐ，正確答案就在題目上。本題的題型是考：until引導的副詞子句修飾前面的動詞片語。

實戰練習

1. After the power outage, chaos would _____ **as people scrambled to find flashlights and candles, and businesses struggled to keep their operations going without electricity.**

   Ⓐ bask   Ⓑ dilate   Ⓒ ensue   Ⓓ probe

2. You should keep your food in _____ conditions. Otherwise, your food may be contaminated with bacteria.

   Ⓐ introductory   Ⓑ biannual   Ⓒ hygienic   Ⓓ presidential

3. Everyone turned to look at John when he walked into the restaurant wearing an _____ outfit **full of colors and decorations.**

   Ⓐ outlandish   Ⓑ insinuating   Ⓒ unresponsive   Ⓓ entrepreneurial

4. Mandy was _____ **when she stood on the edge of cliff, attempting to make her first bungee jumping.**

   Ⓐ venerable   Ⓑ mundane   Ⓒ opulent   Ⓓ petrified

5. In our national forum, there have been several attempts to reform national and institutional rules **with the aim to** _____ **arbitration proceedings.**

   Ⓐ exacerbate   Ⓑ execrate   Ⓒ expedite   Ⓓ extort

6. **Had the plot to massacre the soldiers been carried out**, it could have brought about _____ damage, deaths, and destruction.

   Ⓐ malleable   Ⓑ unfathomable   Ⓒ truculent   Ⓓ vigilant

7. The prime minister's candid admission that his government had accomplished "nothing" and had been lying for "the last year and a half to two years" has _____ the public, **sparking riots in the capital.**

   Ⓐ infuriated   Ⓑ intimidated   Ⓒ improvised   Ⓓ implanted

8. Too much ultraviolet radiation from sunlight, even with sunscreen applied, can actually suppress the immune system, **making you more** _____ **to infection.**

   Ⓐ susceptible   Ⓑ appreciable   Ⓒ combustible   Ⓓ inflammable

9. The employee completed the tedious task _____, **not bothering to put any care or attention to detail into it.**

   Ⓐ fastidiously   Ⓑ morbidly   Ⓒ perfunctorily   Ⓓ succinctly

10. That untamed horse has a ferocious temper; even its owner often saddles up the horse **with** _____.

    Ⓐ trepidation   Ⓑ exhortation   Ⓒ ostentation   Ⓓ constipation

11. The magician's _____ was **so skillful and precise that even the most skeptical audience members were convinced of his supernatural abilities.**

    Ⓐ serendipity   Ⓑ gratification   Ⓒ legerdemain   Ⓓ camaraderie

12. **Being a loyal supporter of the king**, he is a _____ fan of the monarchy.

    Ⓐ fervent   Ⓑ fallow   Ⓒ facetious   Ⓓ fractious

13. The football match turned into a _____ **when the opposing teams began brawling on the field, with players throwing punches and insults and the referee struggling to regain control of the game.**

    Ⓐ lout   Ⓑ goad   Ⓒ fracas   Ⓓ jargon

14. Under his leadership, the company became a(n) _____ acquirer, **absorbing 15 other companies in a mere five years.**

    Ⓐ heterogeneous   Ⓑ fallacious   Ⓒ ravenous   Ⓓ intravenous

15. Eileen Chang explores the claustrophobia of traditional family bonds and the _____ of male-female relationships in a manner so perceptive and modern that many of her fans call her China's Virginia Woolf.

    Ⓐ refurbishment   Ⓑ bifurcation   Ⓒ topography   Ⓓ intricacies

解答

1. Ⓒ 2. Ⓒ 3. Ⓐ 4. Ⓓ 5. Ⓒ 6. Ⓑ 7. Ⓐ 8. Ⓐ 9. Ⓒ 10. Ⓐ
11. Ⓒ 12. Ⓐ 13. Ⓒ 14. Ⓒ 15. Ⓓ

參考書目

Goodman, Kenneth S. (1967). Reading a psycholinguistic guessing game. *Journal of the Reading Specialist*, 6 (1), 126–135.

Halliday, M. A. K., & Hasan, R. (1976). *Cohesion in English*. London: Longman.

Johnson, B. E. (2001). The reading edge: *thirteen ways to build reading comprehension*. Boston: Houghton Mifflin.

King, Burt. (2008). *Practical English grammar and rhetoric*. Taipei: Crane.

Levine, A., Oded, B., & Statman, S. (1988). *Clues to meaning: Strategies for better reading comprehension*. New York: Collier Macmillan.

Paltridge, B. (2006). *Discourse analysis: an introduction*. London: Continuum.

Quirk, R., Greenbaum, S., Leech, G., & Svartvik, J. (1985). *A comprehensive grammar of the English language*. London: Longman.

Strunk, W., & White, E. B. (1999). *The elements of style* (4th ed.). Boston: Allyn and Bacon.

Thompson, G. (2004). *Introducing functional grammar* (2nd.ed.). London: Arnold.

吳潛誠。2017。《中英翻譯：對比分析法（修訂版）》。台北：文鶴。

林連祥。2015。《遠東新世紀英漢辭典》。台北：遠東圖書。

英國劍橋大學出版社。2008。《劍橋高階英漢雙解詞典》。劍橋：劍橋大學出版社。

培生教育出版亞洲有限公司。2013。《朗文當代高級英漢雙解辭典（第五版）》。香港：培生。

莫建清、蔡慈娟、黃素端、洪宜紃、王麗絹、詹惠玲、許凱絨。2011。《英語閱讀Easy Go》。台北：三民。

莫建清。2022。《三民精解英漢辭典》。台北：三民。

莫建清、楊智民、蘇秦、王茹萱。2023。《音義聯想單字記憶法：揭開聲音中的單字密碼，輕鬆找到語音與單字之間的關係，快速擴增英文字彙量》。台北：晨星。

黃自來。1999。《英語詞彙形音義》。台北：文鶴。

黃自來。2017。《應用語言學與英語教學》。台北：書林。

黃宋賢。2022。《超越英文法：大量應用語意邏輯策略，以500則錯誤例示，心智鍛鍊英文認知能力，一掃學習迷思！》。台北：凱信。

霍恩比。2014。《牛津高階英漢雙解詞典（第8版）》。北京：商務印書館。

邁克爾・斯旺。2019。《牛津英語用法指南：第四版》。北京：外語教學與研究。

公務人員高等考試三級考試暨普通考試甄選試題。

各級學校教師甄試獨招試題。

財團法人大學入學考試中心基金會英文指定科目考試試題。

財團法人大學入學考試中心基金會英文學科能力測驗試題。

財團法人技專校院入學測驗中心英文統一入學測驗試題。

各縣市國中、國小教師甄試聯合甄選試題。

教育部受託辦理公立高級中等學校教師甄選測驗試題。

新北市公立高級中等學校教師聯合甄選試題。

碩士班招生考試試題。

學士後（中）醫學系入學招生考試試題。

趣味測試網路走紅 證實漢字順序不一定影響閱讀（民102年5月6日）。中國新聞網。民112年8月4日，取自：https://www.chinanews.com.cn/cul/2013/05-06/4788209.shtml

加入晨星

即享『50元 購書優惠券』

回函範例

您的姓名： 晨小星

您購買的書是： 貓戰士

性別： ●男 ○女 ○其他

生日： 1990/1/25

E-Mail： ilovebooks@morning.com.tw

電話／手機： 09××-×××-×××

聯絡地址： 台中 市 西屯 區
工業區30路1號

您喜歡： ●文學/小說 ●社科/史哲 ●設計/生活雜藝 ○財經/商管
（可複選） ●心理/勵志 ○宗教/命理 ○科普 ○自然 ●寵物

心得分享： 我非常欣賞主角…
本書帶給我的…

"誠摯期待與您在下一本書相遇，讓我們一起在閱讀中尋找樂趣吧！"

國家圖書館出版品預行編目（CIP）資料

英語詞彙語意邏輯解題法（教甄必考版）/莫建清, 楊智民, 黃怡君合著. -- 初版. -- 臺中市：晨星出版有限公司, 2025.04

200面；16.5×22.5公分. -- (語言學習；47)

ISBN 978-626-420-064-6(平裝)

1.CST: 英語 2.CST: 讀本

805.18　　　　　　　　　　　　　　114001056

語言學習 47
英語詞彙語意邏輯解題法（教甄必考版）
只要熟悉詞彙語意邏輯，無論題目如何變化，都能找到答案！

作者	莫建清、楊智民、黃怡君
編輯	余順琪
影片教學	楊智民、黃怡君
封面設計	耶麗米工作室
美術編輯	陳佩幸

創辦人	陳銘民
發行所	晨星出版有限公司 407台中市西屯區工業30路1號1樓 TEL：04-23595820　FAX：04-23550581 E-mail：service-taipei@morningstar.com.tw http://star.morningstar.com.tw 行政院新聞局版台業字第2500號
法律顧問	陳思成律師
初版	西元2025年04月01日

讀者服務專線	TEL：02-23672044／04-23595819#212
讀者傳真專線	FAX：02-23635741／04-23595493
讀者專用信箱	service@morningstar.com.tw
網路書店	http://www.morningstar.com.tw
郵政劃撥	15060393（知己圖書股份有限公司）
印刷	上好印刷股份有限公司

定價 350 元
（如書籍有缺頁或破損，請寄回更換）
ISBN：978-626-420-064-6

Published by Morning Star Publishing Inc.
Printed in Taiwan
All rights reserved.
版權所有・翻印必究

｜最新、最快、最實用的第一手資訊都在這裡｜